W0010162

An Anglo-American Alliance: A Serio-Comic Romance And Forecast Of The Future

Gregory Casparian

In the interest of creating a more extensive selection of rare historical book reprints, we have chosen to reproduce this title even though it may possibly have occasional imperfections such as missing and blurred pages, missing text, poor pictures, markings, dark backgrounds and other reproduction issues beyond our control. Because this work is culturally important, we have made it available as a part of our commitment to protecting, preserving and promoting the world's literature. Thank you for your understanding.

An
Anglo-American Alliance

A Serio-Comic Romance
and
Forecast of the Future

BY

GREGORY CASPARIAN

———

*Illustrated and Published by
the Author*

———

Mayflower Press
Floral Park, New York
1906

Copyrighted, 1906,
by
GREGORY CASPARIAN

All Rights Reserved

Table of Contents

Foreword

IN presenting this volume to the public it is not
the intention of the author to offer it as a literary masterpiece, but, in his adopted language—conscious of his limitation—merely to give expression
to his thoughts on certain problems of life that have
always seemed to him of particular significance.

At present there appears to be a general bombas-
tic clamor among certain nations who, decrying
others as barbarous, claim to have reached the highest pinnacle of civilization. Yet a glance at the existing conditions in those self-lauded governments
will reveal rampant corruption among their leaders
who, for their own selfish ends, *retard legislations*
which are absolutely imperative for the general welfare. It is not necessary to mention other ways in
which the people are being daily betrayed, for this is
sufficient to render any thinking person despondent
and pessimistic.

The causes of the decadence of nations are not
the laws which have been enacted, but the flagrant
violation of these very laws, actuated by greed, avarice
and commercialism which are generated in the individual in power. The only remedy for this state
is either a leader of intrepid courage or the awaken-

ing of the people themselves and their demanding reforms by public mandate.

The true meaning of civilization is Universal Brotherhood, and in this sense, the leading lights in every stratum of life, whether in Government or in Commerce, in Religion or in Science, stand arraigned and indicted before the tribunal of conscience for retarding this laudable spirit of Brotherhood.

Why do not Captains of Industry and Commerce, instead of throttling each other, by a unanimous effort, promulgate laws on a reciprocal basis among themselves?

Why do not Scientists, instead of confining their efforts to individual endeavors, combine their forces so as to enhance the chance of accomplishing greater results in research and exploration?

Why do not Spiritual Shepards, instead of preaching intolerance and fanaticism, bring their flocks together in harmony? An Oriental scholar in the Congress of Religions, at the Columbian Fair, declared that "the flocks are willing to pasture together, but it is the shepards who are keeping them apart."

And in fine, why do not the Nations, each claiming the highest forms of civilization, instead of disseminating national, sectional and race hatred, form an alliance, which will advance the cause of Universal Brotherhood, and brighten the hope of bringing enduring peace to the world at large?

In this golden era, with its vast numbers of diplomats, statemen, theologians, scientists, and its countless fraternal organizations,—each preaching, fraternity, love and charity,—what evil spirit or genii prevents them from forming a union between two of

the foremost and best forms of Governments,—
America and Britain—perfect types in their entity,
having similar laws, language and aspirations?

Who will be the Savior, through whose agency
this happy cross fertilization, inoculation or union
shall be achieved? It was the above thoughts, and
the idea of an alliance between COLUMBIA and
BRITANNIA, that suggested in all seriousness the
following frivolously allegorical narrative,—a *pot-
pourri* of weird fancy, satire and imagination, a
mosaic of the sublime and the ridiculous, on themes
worthy of a master.

Yet if some reader should find, even in this fantastic guise, an occasional thought worthy of arousing
him to nobler efforts, the author will consider himself well rewarded.

In regard to his prophecies for the future, he is
willing to be called a consummate prevaricator
should his desire for the betterment of mankind or
the unity of nations take place much sooner than he
has predicted, or the calamities fail to materialize or
prove to be much lighter than he has foreseen.

G. C.

Floral Park, N. Y.

CHAPTER I

The Young Ladies' Seminary

IT is 1960, Anno Domini. The Earth, notwithstanding many dire predictions of charlatans and religious fanatics, and in spite of numerous cataclysms, conflagrations and political upheavals, was rotating serenely on its axis.

The Diana Young Ladies' Seminary, situated upon the picturesque hills of Cornwall on the Hudson, is a few miles north of the West Point Military Academy. The seminary buildings, having formerly been the palatial homestead of a multi-millionaire, about half a century previously had been bequeathed to the State of New York, with ample endowments for its maintenance and development. It had long since become one of the finest institutions of learning of its kind, not only of America, but of the whole civilized world.

The donor of this magnificent seat of knowl-

edge for young ladies was a man of " polarity,"
of positive and negative action and reaction.
He was in fact a typical incarnation and em-
bodiment of a dualism, immortalized by the
fertile fancy of Robert Louis Stevenson, in his
story of " Dr. Jekyll and Mr. Hyde."   While
on the one hand he had an apparently irresistible and monomaniacal cunning in robbing
his fellow men by monopolizing all the necessities of life, crushing with hellish unscrupulousness all competition in every channel of
industry, and strewing his wake with industrial wrecks,—on the other hand he busied himself with the erection of hospitals and churches,
and in endowing colleges with a princely lib-
erality, commensurate to his other nature.

Emerson, the philosopher, says " The whole
universe is so, and so every one of its parts,"
that " an inevitable dualism bisects nature,"
each thing being a half and suggesting its
complement.   As the mammoth Californian
redwood tree, which with its towering height
looks overpoweringly stupendous when compared with the tiny otaheite orange or dwarf
Japanese plant, so was the difference in power
of acquisitiveness and possibilities of dispensa-

tion between this colossus compared with ordinary mortals.

The real motive of his charity could not be
divined; whether it was because, pricked by a
guilty conscience, he used this means as a pal-
liative for his sins, or whether he was entirely
oblivious of wrong-doing and was prompted
only by a frank desire for doing good, was
never determined.   But at any rate after his
death it was found that he had donated his
palaces, with munificent endowment funds, to
establish this educational institution for fe-
males.   Moreover, it is not my intention to
write a biography of this dual monster of
money-maniac and philanthropist, for his deeds
are written on the graves and sorrowing hearts
of his victims, as well as in the grateful re-
membrance and esteem of his beneficiaries.

Besides, we are told that God works good
even through the agency of the devil, and if
he really had been a satellite of Satan, the
great usefulness and wide influence for good of
the Seminary demonstrated the veracity of the
above statement.

The Diana Seminary had proven its right to
its high place in the public esteem.   Its fame

had reached every corner of the earth. Young women, not only from America but from every clime and nation, flocked thither seeking to perfect themselves in such branches of education as are the necessary requirements of the fair sex to fit them to reign supreme in any capacity, from teaching in a country school to presiding on regal thrones and guiding the destinies of Nations.

The Diana Seminary had become particularly famous for the especial branches of a curriculum which rendered the young ladies magnificently lovely in form, chic in habilaments, brilliant and vivacious in conversation, serene and dignified in carriage, sweet and optimistic in nature, pure in sentiments, and in addition conferred upon them all the necessary qualifications of accomplished housewives, virtues all of which are inherent in American women and susceptible of highest development.

The graduates of this Seminary were always eagerly sought in marriage, not only by the deserving young men living near the college, but also by the nobility and even the royalty of Europe. The demands of the latter class were indeed so great as to alarm the fond parents across the ocean for the future happiness of their daughters, and they were thus compelled to send their beloved ones to this Institution in order to acquire that polish which their American sisters had proven so desirable.

Amongst the many English maidens who were there matriculated was beautiful Aurora Cunningham, the only daughter of the Secretary of Foreign affairs of Great Britain.

It is unnecessary to dwell upon the beauty and charms of Aurora. It is true that she could not be compared with the Goddesses of ancient Greece, nor did she resemble the bewitching sylvan nymphs depicted by the brush and pen of masters of art. She was a mortal; suffice it to say, that she was a graceful girl of exquisitely moulded form, of medium height, with luxuriant golden tresses, which, shimmering in the sunlight, justified her baptismal name. Her large, dreamy blue eyes mirrored the purity of her soul, and the dimples on her cheeks were so deep and alluring that all who looked upon them felt their compelling charm.

She was, in a word, a typical English maiden. Highly accomplished, and though dainty in demeanor, nevertheless she was not one of those frail, ailing butterflies who exist and thrive only in artificial atmosphere. Having been reared with greatest care, by means of a complete course of calisthenics and out-of-door sports, with all her refined mien she was a hardy and healthy specimen of feminine beauty as well as a leader in all the strenuous pastimes of the Diana Seminary.

She was called the " sunshine " of the Seminary, and none other merited the appellation so well. Consequently she was idolized by the rest of the students and was much sought after by the gallant young men in the vicinity. After the manner of girl students who are given to violent friendships, Aurora was devoted to her room-mate in the person of a charming American girl named Margaret MacDonald, the daughter of a Western Senator.

Margaret was entirely the opposite of Aurora, —her very antithesis. She was somewhat taller, with sparkling black eyes and raven hair, of imposing dignity and carriage, but withal the equal of Aurora in the matter of natural gifts and accomplishments. She had, moreover, a captivating frivolity and aggressiveness which almost bordered on masculinity.

Perhaps it was this complete diversity of temperament and of type that engendered an intense affinity between the girls. For although diametrically differing even in their exposition of ideas, they were drawn to each other with a mysterious sympathy which attracted the attention of outsiders and furnished ample excuse for comment. Directly after their first meeting they had become inseparable companions and confidants.

As the time passed this strange attachment grew so marked and its manifestations so alarmingly flagrant that they themselves became aware of its dangerous consequences. They realized that if they gave free license to indiscreet emotional demonstrations in the class room or in public, not only would their actions not be tolerated by the College faculty and cause their expulsion from the Seminary, but they would also be subjected to unendurable ostracism by the rest of the students. But still worse was the confronting fact that they would undoubtedly become the topic of unpleasant notoriety through the publicity given by the sensational press. They had therefore the good judgment to pledge themselves to control their emotions in the presence of the class, and to exercise wide-awake circumspection in their behavior in public and towards the opposite sex.

It is needless to say that by the happy faculty of diplomacy, inherent in them, they succeeded with consummate delicacy and skill in maintaining their natural poise and normal attitude throughout the seminary course.

Like the magnetic pole the Diana Seminary had become the center of attraction for the adjacent youths, especially the Academy boys, who on all gala occasions were welcome guests at the Seminary.

The experiment of co-education had long since been proven a failure. By the well known law of electricity, that bodies similarly electrified repel each other, and bodies oppositely electrified attract, it seems that the constant familiarity and co-mingling of the two sexes in co-educational institutions at the romantic age of puberty had a somewhat similar effect and breeded contempt, blunting that keen fondness for each other which seems natural, and so was not surprising that in such institutions both sexes, when leaving college, separated more like enemies than friends and lovers.

The isolation of the sexes naturally created an intensity of affection and a desire for association, and when the two periodically came in contact caused that rapturous thrill of hearts and nascent unification of souls. This undoubtedly was the plausible explanation, at least one of the reasons, why the Seminary girls were always in demand and were participants of so many happy unions.

The only exception to the rule were Aurora and Margaret who, although in every way agreeable to the aspirants for their hearts and hands, refrained from making an alliance throughout their college course. It was piteously amusing, however, to see those gallant swains from the Academy heading for the Seminary whenever opportunity presented. Their hearts were filled with intense ardor and their lips and pubescent moustaches were pregnant with the microbes of Eros,—in a high state of fermentation—blurting out with tense anxiety the momentous query, " Wilt thou be mine?" to Aurora or Margaret, only to return vanquished by the cold decisive negative.

CHAPTER II

The Initiation

THERE was no cause for ennui at the Diana Seminary. Notwithstanding the serious course of study, there was ample jollity. The tedium of their leisure hours was beguiled with all kinds of recreations according to the seasons of the year.

There were the various Seminary teams in basket ball, fencing, golfing, calisthenics and amateur theatricals. The girls also indulged in excursions to the exhibitions of the Academy boys, on their gala days of mimic warfare in the campus, as well as to their contests on the diamond or gridiron at foot ball. This latter sport having reached in those days the top notch of perfection, it furnished the fair spectators thrills of excitement when the contestants in their improved steel helmets and cuirass, with pronged leggings and spiked shoes looked like veritable knights of the chivalric ages. It

A " Full-Back " in 1960

gave an additional source of lingering pleasure
and admiration at such contests when half a
dozen ambulances were required to cart away
the gladiators in *hors du combat.*

Besides all the above recreations, the Seminary girls had also their various secret organizations which furnished ample work for winter
months. One of the most notable of these fra-
ternities was called the D. N. A.; signifying
"Daughters of the New Alliance."

A brief description of the sacred rites of this
unique fraternity, on an interesting initiation,
may not here be amiss. It took place during
the incumbency of the two principal organizers and charter members—Aurora and Margaret,—the latter occupying at the time the most
exalted position of Reverend High Priestess
and the former that of Supreme Guide. The
initiation in question was remarkable for the
singular coincidence that the applicants for
membership were discovered to be of half a
dozen nationalities—French, German, Scotch,
Irish, Italian and Hebrew,—and this unusual
circumstance lent the occasion widespread sensation among the other members and made the
session most memorable.

A peep in the temple revealed a bewildering spectacle, an " Adamless Eden " of loveliness as it were. Margaret MacDonald, enveloped in gorgeously embroidered Grecian robes, enthroned on an elevated dais, a golden sceptre in hand, and a brilliant diadem on her shapely head, presented an imposing figure as High Priestess, while Aurora in a tight fitting cuirass of variegated spangles, holding a trident, performed her official duties.   Other functionaries attired in chaste Grecian costumes occupied their respective positions.

In the proscenium the applicants, attired in their respective national costumes, followed the assistant guide to the gate of the temple when, on pressing a button, an extremely melodious chant surged through the atmosphere.   This called the attention of the Supreme Guide to the fact that there were applicants for membership. The Supreme Guide in the same manner then made the announcement to the high priestess, and the latter commanded them to be admitted to the temple. At the clanking of the cymbals and the sounding of the fanfares as if by magic the gate was ajar, revealing to the eyes of the new disciples a dazzling scene of harmoniously blended loveliness. They filed in and arranged themselves in the shape of a crescent at the lower end of the temple.

In the centre of the room, on an alabaster table, they could discern a glass receptacle in which, squirming and wriggling, were a quantity of angle worms; on another similar table close by they could see a golden cage, wherein half a dozen tiny rodents were playing tag. In one corner a fierce, pugnacious billy-goat was butting with vicious vigor against one of the Grecian columns of the temple.

When the sound of the fanfares subsided the High Priestess, rising suddenly and striking three times on the marble floor with her magic sceptre, commanded silence, and in a sweet voice spoke thus:

"Supreme Guide of the order of D. N. A. what bringest thou to this sanctuary?"

The guide answered in pathetic tones: "Thou High Priestess of the order of D. N. A., I bring thee greeting. I bring thee also jewels rare, for thy shrine; gems, not still life or crystals petrified, but forms divine, animate with heaving breasts, with radiant brows, and sparkling eyes that volumes speak, that even Cupid, dazed, would soon forget his ancient Psyche fair, and yet unable be whom amongst these for himself to take."

" Have they signified their willingness to be tested for courage and fortitude ?"

" They have."

" Are they ready to travel through the tortuous path of the inquisition ?"

" They are."

"Then prithee, take them to the ante-chamber that their eyes may be blindfolded and the robes of chastity may be thrown over them. Then bring them thither through the tortuous path of the inquisition to my presence."

Accordingly they were taken to the ante-room and while being prepared for the journey they were given plain intimation that they were to make a repast of the angle worms and fondly handle the young rodents, while direct hints of riding the bellicose goat were thrown out, as though this were the least of the test to which they were to be subjected.

Preparation for their return to the Temple being completed, their readiness was again communicated as before and to the solemn but inspiring Andante of Faust they began to wind through a path of serpentine evolutions. On their journey many strange and threatening voices came to their ears, some cursing their undertaking and advising them to return before too late, some whispering that they were about to step into an abyss or to encounter dire disaster. But by the guidance and occasional prod by the trident of timid and erratic disciples they proceeded onward with cautious steps. When almost at the end of their journey, however, there was a sharp cry from one of the applicants which caused the procession to halt.

Lady Rosa Redmont Davitt, the daughter of an Irish noble,—a comely girl, with laughing eyes, full of wit and humor and with a strong combative instinct, withal very popular at the seminary—gave vent to her distress in a piquant but pleasing accent:

"Ouch! Your Riverence," said she, "It is not that I moind to ride the wild billy goat, or am afraid to swallow the serpints, but divil a bit I can shtand this pinching of my goide, your Riverince; my back is almost bhlack and bhlue."

"It is well that thou hast spoken," said the

Priestess; " it was because of thy untractable erratic steps and non-susceptibility to the promptings of thy guide that thou hast suffered, for according to the ratio of the loyalty and sensitiveness to her touch, thy sufferings will come to an end.   Follow thou, then, fair maid, with keen perception to the subtle touch of thy guide.   Supreme Guide of the order of D. N. A. let the procession proceed."

The march having been resumed and finished, they stood thus blindfolded before the High Priestess in order to be tested for courage and fortitude.   Each applicant was led by the guide before her, who, for fortitude, administered the angle worm, and for courage trailed the mouse over their limbs.   It is perhaps unnecessary to mention that macaroni was substituted for the angle worm and that an artificial mouse served as a lively rodent.

When these sacred and solemn rites were performed the applicants were taken through numerous evolutions of a march to the centre of the room, in front of a table, whereon rested in the folds of American and British colors the Constitution and By-laws of the Order.   There the oath of Allegiance was administered and at a thunderous outburst of music, the bandages were cut asunder and the applicants found themselves in the glow of a diffused light. Standing in the middle of the room, surrounded by rows of graceful girls arrayed in immaculate Grecian costumes, were all the other members of the Order. While the High Priestess, majestically waving her sceptred arm, proclaimed them tried and true members of D. N. A.

The ceremonies were concluded by the singing of the National Anthems.

CHAPTER III

The Moonlight Soiree

MARGARET was reclining on a divan in her luxurious study, perusing a letter. The room was redolent with the perfume of June roses, and the warm rays of the afternoon sun, filtering through the stained glass windows —now and then obscured by the swaying leaves and branches of the trees—were flitting across her lovely form as if playing hide and seek.

Suddenly the door burst open and Aurora, somewhat flushed, holding in her hand a note, entered the room, exclaiming excitedly:

"Horrible! Margie, horrible! I do not know what to do! It will be extremely h'embawassing aw, don't you know."

"What is it Aurora, is that Jewsky after you again?"* asked Margaret with a rougish smile, glancing toward her chum.

* The slang in vogue half a century ago may be found now in standard dictionaries. Its use was considered in good form by the elite of that day.

28

"Is the Jewski After You Again?"

"I do not think he is a 'Ebrew, my dear, his signature aw, is some foreign sounding name. Carlos Do-Do-Do-Don Seville."

"Well, I don't care what he is. The dodo is an extinct bird you know. He looks like a Jewsky anyway. The idea, pray what has he to say?" questioned Margaret, contracting her eyebrows to a frown.

"He writes that he will grace aw, our moonlight reception with 'is presence. Horrid, Margie, horrid! I hate him!"

"Fiddlesticks! Rats!" retorted Margaret. "It is up to us then. If he bobs up tomorrow night at the show, there will be something doing. That Dago is positively the limit. He is perfectly horrid. If I see him ogling me once that night, I'll 'cut the chains of my tongue loose' at him, the wretch!"

"Aw, really, how brave you are Margie!" replied Aurora, looking admiringly at her classmate. "You will not desert me? By the way," went on Aurora, gradually recovering her composure, "I just met Norma Southworth coming from the modiste with her graduation gown. It was such a bonnie gown, aw, so lurid and so sweet, don't you know."

"I bet you hers won't cut any ice with my togs, when they arrive tomorrow. Aurora, you and I will make a jim-dandy pair on graduation day. I am curious, however, to get a glimpse of her dream of a gown, but before we start, my dear, let us once more go over the details of tomorrow night's event."

"It makes me somewhat nervous to think about it. I wish truly it was all h'over, Margie."

"So do I, Aurora. I am afraid we'll make a beastly flunk at the show, aren't you?"

"Bah Jove, it will be awfully dweddful, Margie, to make a failure, after so many months of preparation. I hope we will come h'out all right," said Aurora with thoughtful anxiety.

After they finished their examination of the program, both started out to inspect Norma's gown, intending from thence to go to the final rehearsal. While crossing the Grand Court of the Seminary they spied Professor Cielo Allenson coming toward them on his motor-cycle.

"There comes the dear "Old Guard" said Aurora. "Isn't 'e a dear, aw, isn't 'e sweet?"

"To be sure Aurora, I am head over heels

in love with his lilacs; aren't they elegant?" was the ready rejoinder of Margaret.

"Eh, what! aw, really, 'ow often must I caution you not to use such h'expressions," said Aurora, reproachfully. "'E may 'ear you, Margie, 'e may 'ear you."

"There, ring off, sweet child, you better pick up your 'h's' and get a gait on, or else we'll be late for practice," laughed Margaret.

".Oh, how do you do?" piped both girls.

The professor, slackening his pace, greeted them courteously: "I presume you ladies are well prepared for the ordeal of tomorrow night?"

"Quite so, Professor; we are looking forward with extreme pleasure to meeting our gallant adversaries under your charge," answered Margaret.

"H'in fact, we are now going to our final rehearsal," added Aurora.

"Well, I wish you success, ladies; I must be off myself, to give the boys at the Academy my last instructions; so goodby."

"Good afternoon, Professor; goodby."

        *   *   *   *

The June graduation day of 1960 at the

Seminary was not far distant, falling on the second week of the month. The recitations had been discontinued and the only sessions that were held by the professors were chiefly for purposes of review.

The students meanwhile beguiled their time by indulging in frequent class receptions, which were given by the various grades and societies, each vieing with others to excel all previous functions in originality, splendor and novelty. That to be given by the senior class, to which Aurora and Margaret belonged, was near at hand. Long before the date agreed upon, the senior class had agreed to make it an out-of-door affair eclipsing all previous efforts in brilliancy of conception and prodigality of arrangements.

It was to be a "Soiree Artistique!" a Tableau Vivant Extravaganza! followed by a moonlight dance and reception. Their guests of honor were to be no less than embryo generals from the West Point Military Academy! Truly it was a magnificent conception and it was chiefly due to the indefatigable efforts of Aurora and Margaret that it culminated in a stupendous success with the night of the open air Fête.

The spacious, velvety lawn was profusely and fittingly decorated. From column to column festoons of June roses and evergreens crossed and entwined in bewildering array. The colossal statue of Diana with her hounds —the patron Saint of the Seminary—and the alternate gold and silver peristyles leading to the wondrously designed parterre, were enveloped in a mass of phosphorescent glow from the radium globules.

The statuettes and fountains were bejewelled by innumerable actinium bulbs. Ensconced in the branches of the trees and bushes the electrical nightingales gave forth their continuous warbles of subdued sweetness, while from poles especially erected for the occasion electric globes in kaleidoscopic hues diffused the ambient atmosphere with their spirituelle glow. The moon, like an overseer, hung high in the canopy of space, casting its silvery light over the radiant scene.

The graceful figures of the maidens in their fantastic winged costumes of Celestial Amazons, and the grotesque forms of the boys, attired in Indian outfits, glittering with beads and feathers—" chaperoned " by the venerable

Professor Cielo Allenson—each tribe in turn illustrating their weird national customs, in war or peace, in mirth or sorrow, filled the select spectators with throes of thrilling excitement. What hitherto had seemed only ordinary, mundane surroundings was changed into a realistic happy-hunting-ground or savage fairyland, a vision of alternate celestial or barbaric splendor, the grandeur of which is beyond the power of human ability to describe.

The secret of unparalleled excellence of the disguises of the boys was due to the fact that at the end of the Freshmen year at the Military Academy, when they were preparing for the celebration of their academic year, the Sophomores had kidnapped the whole Freshmen Class, and by a pre-arranged plan, experts having been hired, had tatooed them all over their faces as Indians on the warpath, thus leaving a lasting souvenir of class antagonism ! Being disfigured for life, they had made the best of their misfortune by appearing in the role of Indian warriors, delighted that for once this misfortune had proven an advantage.

There was nothing to mar this auspicious occasion except that, near its close, a trivial wordy demonstration took place between Professor Cielo Allenson and an intruder named Carlos Don Seville.

Still, even the most pleasant and successful events have their aftermath and this affair left several of them. When Aurora and Margaret entered their rooms heaped with triumphant compliments for their consummate skill in planning this grand farewell féte they were sad, sad through an impulsive intuition.

Hardly had they crossed the threshold of their room when they fell into each other's arms, sobbing bitterly from the bottom of their hearts. Each instinctively knew why the other wept. The final class reception had a deep significance to them, as it meant that graduation day was near at hand. In the natural course of events each would now go her way to a distant home. It meant separation!

Separation! It was impossible for them calmly to accept the full significance of that word in their infatuation for each other. Some time elapsed before either gained sufficient composure to speak. Each attempt resulted in a collapse and a paroxysm of hysterical weeping.

LIBRARY OF THE UNIVERSITY OF CALIFORNIA

Margaret, as if dazed with the frenzy of that strange passion, clung to Aurora, exclaiming hysterically: "How can it be, Aurora? It cannot be. It cannot be! Better death than separation!"

By the gentle, soothing words of Aurora, however, they gradually recovered their composure, but were not fully pacified until that very night they made a solemn compact, bound by an inviolable oath, not to make any alliance with any suitor whatever and to remain united to each other in souls until death should them part.

It was that night also that in the height of their fatuous ardor of love Aurora wrote an impromptu poem of fealty, entitled "Wilt Thou Remember Thy Vow?" It revealed the intensity of their emotions, their utter subjugation and mutual abandonment of will and desire each to the other and its dire revenge in the end, if their solemn vow was betrayed.

Like the poem, the music which was composed by Margaret, was also an inspiration. It interpreted the poem in a sad, sublimely pathetic strain, yet at times in bold and threatening torrents of color and passion. The very spirit of the words and the oath, that would be their guiding star throughout their lives, surged through it. In all respects it was a masterpiece of symphonic creation.

CHAPTER IV

Historical Events of the 20th Century

THE senior class of the Diana Seminary were assembled in the auditorium, listening in a trance of respectful attention to Professor Cielo Allenson. He had just begun his review of the historical events of the 20th Century, now and then giving his individual comments upon the subjects presented.

1900

An Era of False Prosperity

With the beginning of the 20th Century was inaugurated an era of false prosperity. The Census Bureau at that time furnishes statistics and comments upon the wonderfully perceptible decrease of the criminal classes, called foot-pads, sneak thieves and highwaymen, which was attributed chiefly to the existing national prosperity. It overlooks the fact, however, that a new species of miscreants, comparatively more dangerous, had begun to thrive like mushrooms in prolific numbers,—that of so-called *commercial brigands* or *financial buccaneers* who, under fascinating and attractive names, such as mining syndicates with their fabulous deposits of gold, offering bucketfuls of shares for a dime ; banking and building loan associations, with palatial homes thrown in gratis to every subscriber; promoters of illusionary inventions, seeking shareholders, which would make them millionaires in the twinkling of an eye.

Alchemists who, with their artful empyrics of legerdemain, transmuted base metals into gold, and were willing to dispose of their precious wares for pennies; Wall Street and race-track spiders posing as benevolent philanthropists, scattering fortunes right and left to every applicant, sapped the avaricious, sottish public of its dearly bought earnings. Strange to say, despite many colossal exposures and failures, as these adroit swindlers grew more subtle and audacious, the more the gambling-crazed public rushed to their destruction.

The effect was appalling. In consequence

of the depredations of these pirates of industries, the reputable business and financial firms were the greatest sufferers. Their legitimate transactions were paralyzed to such a tremendous degree that they were compelled to devise ways and means to counteract its evils. In 1908, after mature deliberation at a general convention in Washington, it was decided to raise ample funds and create a bureau under the auspices of the Federal Government called the *Bureau of Frauds and Swindles.* The duties imposed upon its officers were the ferreting out and prosecuting of the wild-cat schemes and to warn the public against them.

The measure, being approved by the National Government, had the desired effect of freeing to a great degree the financial world from its parasites of industrial malefactors, and to some extent established again the stability and integrity of honorable financiers, in the meanwhile safeguarding foolish persons from being fleeced out of their savings.

1902
The Cataclysm at Martinique

St. Pierre, Martinique, was destroyed by a volcanic eruption of Mount Peleé, on the eighth day of May. In a few minutes more than thirty thousand human beings were hurled into eternity.

1908

The Mormon Question

The anti-plural wives laws were enforced to the letter. Its emphatic application to all members of the sect was brought about principally by the Women's Clubs, whose persistent and overwhelming aggressiveness played an important factor in the stamping out of this demoralizing and materialistic religion. In this era of civilization the existence of a religious organization of this character, like a cancerous growth, was threatening to debase womanhood and lead the communities to unbridled licentiousness.

1909

Capital and Labor

Every new movement, be it religious, political or economic, has its birth like a volcano, and unionism was no exception to this rule. The labor unions at first had their violent agitators who, possessing greater physical than mental calibre, laid the crude foundation of a force in an arbitrary manner that consequently had its gradual evolution of development.

Their constant conflicts with capital were characterized by an unreasonable amount of physical argument which resulted in more or less disastrous denouements, but these very acts of lawlessness and disturbances awakened·a third party, the consumers in general, who were equally affected by the disturbances between capital and labor and brought about a realization of the true relative positions.

Labor certainly has its unalienable rights and was entitled to due consideration and justice. However, like the negative and positive poles of electricity, which are both essential in order that a circuit of effective force be generated, capital and labor likewise had their dual relative values of importance, without which there could be no constancy of harmonious production.

By the gradual awakening of both capital and labor to their true limitations, the questions involved began to assume a more intelligent basis under the codes of arbitration. At the same time the violent agitators of labor were succeeded in the trend of this onward development by more intelligent organizers. These latter were merged into accomplished, rational leaders and, through the efficient medium of the ballot box, into national representatives. Consequently, the more dignified, orderly and responsible labor became, the more the workers became entitled to the benefits of their labor.

A Department of Capital and Labor which, so far, had been merely probationary now became a permanent institution at the Capitol and in every State of the Union as well.

1910
The Expense of Living

It is one of the strangest inconsistencies of social problems, that although political economists and scholars have preached the doctrine, that inventions and improved methods in mechanical lines contribute to the blessings of mankind by cheapening the necessities of life, yet in spite of their plausible declarations, the cost of living year by year grew higher and higher, entailing untold suffering and despair among the poorer classes.

The cause of this lamentable perversion was

due to a certain clique of unscrupulous progeny of Mammon, called trusts and corporations, who, being blinded with an insatiable desire for pelf and lust, and stupefied with a frenzied avarice, monopolized all the necessities of life. The vast occidental domain of our country was of unlimited resources and was capable of producing in abundance the products which they " cornered." The *modus operandi* of their rapacious operations were manifold. They limited the output of Nature's bounty in order to keep them at prohibitive values, and at the same time deprived hosts of sons of toil of earning their livelihood. They kept at their inoperative mercy—by their abominable tactics of purchase—the producer from receiving his just share, and they also mulcted the helpless consumer by the unlimited inflation of their capital stock and fictitious expenses until at length the burden of their avarice became unendurable.

Although attempts have repeatedly been made by sincere executives of the Nation, by the advocation of measures for curbing the rapacity of these trusts, their endeavors met with failure on account of the vague and flex-

ible laws already in existence, and by the array of sycophantic traitors in high circles who
prevented any legislation which was conducive
to the tranquility and welfare of the masses.
At last, only after a series of sanguinary demonstrations by the people which almost endan-
gered the stability of the republic, they were
compelled to yield.

By the passage of clearly defined laws the
career of their nefarious system of spoliation
was brought to an end. One of the most effi-
cacious laws passed was the creation of a body
of competent men of supreme power who
appraised approximately the capitalization of
these concerns and licensed them as such under oath. The States in the meantime assumed the power of fixing a maximum value
for which their commodities might be placed
on the market. By the above legislations the
inflation of their capital and extortion from
the consumer were made securely impossible.

1911
Death of an Eminent Scholar

Professor Henry Richfield, a profound scholar, and the author of " How to Get Rich "—a

ponderous work in twelve octavo volumes—
passed away in an attic, in abject penury and
squalor.

1912
The Annihilation of Mosquitoes

Although the mortality statistics in the
United States for last year reached the round
number of two million persons from various
diseases, among them chiefly from consump-
tion, pneumonia, typhoid fever and epidemics
of smallpox and diphtheria, a few sporadic
cases of death were recorded resulting from
mosquito bites, which gave grave concern to
the medical fraternity.

The outcome of this alarm was the calling
of a general conference of bacteriological experts. The mosquito, that had hitherto enjoyed unbridled freedom since the creation of
his race, was now looked upon as the arch
enemy of mankind. A noted philanthropist,
interested in oil wells and having on hand a
great bulk of unmarketable crude petroleum,
donated a large sum for research in order to
discover ways and means of curbing the rav-
ages of these nefarious pests which threatened
the annihilation of the human race.

It was decided by the savants, that the distribution of crude petroleum in stagnant pools and humid marshes, was the only effective method for the extermination of mosquito life. The distribution of greenbacks for their valuable services, (notwithstanding the fact that under the microscope they were found to contain two hundred and fifty-seven diseases and thirty-eight million microbes to the square inch), were grabbed with unprecedented avidity by these same specialists.

1913
Child Labor

The dwarfing and crippling of the mental, moral and physical growth of tender children, by the avaricious employers, and its baleful consequence of peopling the community with moral and bodily degenerates, devoid of the desirable elements of good citizenship, had become so appallingly flagrant that a general sentiment of the people was aroused in a mighty protest to the Federal authorities.

Thanks to the aggressive and strenuons legislative warfare of Labor Unions in every State, aided by the persistent moral agitation of Women's Clubs all over the country, child labor was entirely abolished in many channels of industries, such as mills, factories, collieries and plantations.   In more gentle occupations the employment of minors, was placed on a healthier and more humane basis than had ever before been the case.

1914
The Great Radium Swindle

The fabulously high price of this metal had awakened the cupidity of a coterie of adroit schemers who, had palmed off on unsuspecting men of science, a rank substitute which cost only a trifle to manufacture.

After securing an enormous sum of money, the schemers had decamped to parts unknown.

It was discovered that the spurious metal thus disposed was nothing more than a highly compressed form of phosphorous.

1915
Death of an Eminent Physician

Dr. Wisehardt, the brilliant young physician and surgeon who discovered the electro-magnetic germ-cells of life, and invented methods to prolong life itself by the cultivation of these cells, died in the 27th year of his age from premature senility.

1916
A Tidal Wave

The most memorable event of this year was a gigantic tidal wave of tremendous height, which swept over the lower coast of Florida. In a few minutes it inundated and destroyed a vast area of the coast, doing incalculable damage to shipping. It was estimated that nearly fifteen thousand persons lost their lives in this cataclysm.

1917
War Between United States and Columbia

The stubborn attitude of the Central American Republic, Columbia, towards the United States, by her menacing antagonism to the construction of the interoceanic canal, gradually created a breach of the peace that led ultimately to a forcible demonstration by the United States, and precipitated the invasion by the latter of the Republic of Panama.

Peace was re-established after a crushing defeat of the Columbians. The famous waterway, the Republic of Panama, then became United States territory, by annexation.

1918
The Women's Clubs

The Women's Clubs which, during their first inception, were the subject of much ridicule, and the proceedings of their meetings a theme for ribald jokes in the secular press, gradually developed into such gigantic proportions that their influence became a powerful factor in every public question of the day, and in fact so continues unabated unto this day.

The last Federal statistics show more than two thousand Institutions in the form of sanitariums, refuges, technical schools of practical utility, entirely under the auspices of Club Women. The constitutions of these laudable organizations " invariably stand for something which is ennobling " and their achievements are monumental tributes to the upward trend of womanhood.

There was, however, a crucial period in their affairs worth mentioning. Some of these noble but over-zealous women of that period, in their exuberant enthusiasm for woman's rights, forgetting the limitations of their sex,—considered by the greatest thinkers of the past ages to be the sphere of Home,—agitated a propaganda of political equality or suffrage and, from time to time, created a stir among their organizations until at last, in 1918, the National Federation of Women's Clubs decided to hold a conclave in order to decide the following momentous question: "Should Women Enter Politics?"

More than four thousand five hundred delegates from all over the Union assembled at Madison Square Garden, in New York City. Sympathizers of the suffragists with their eloquence tried to railroad through a measure in their behalf, but equally able leaders of the opposition—benefitted by the warning of Sages —succeeded in counterbalancing the efforts of their fair antagonists.

After a heated symposium the question was put to a vote, which resulted decisively in a victory for those who opposed the movement. It was further voted, that they should confine all their energies to civic, educational and humanitarian channels and things pertaining to Home. This was a most happy and wise decision, for the world at large needs mothers who will beget and nurse a Florence Nightingale, a Clara Barton, a Washington or a Lincoln, rather than mothers who would become a Jezebel, a Delilah or a Cleopatra.

1919
The Tornado

A cyclonic tornado of intense velocity and destructive force struck New York City, demolishing in its path, in the shape of a semicircle from the Battery to Twenty-third Street, West, two hundred and seventy-five buildings. Fortunately, the day being a holiday, the loss of life was comparatively small.

1920
The Power of the Press

Through emancipation from its shackles of monarchic censorship and subserviency to despotic masters, the upward rise of the Press to usefulness and power was without a parallel— a power to which even Napoleon Bonaparte was sensible when he said, "I fear three newspapers more than a hundred thousand bayonets." But like everything else in the universe, the Press also had its dual potentiality.

Like a two-edged sword, it could be wielded
for good or evil. In the hands of an unscrupulous politician it was a treacherous weapon,
while in the control of the righteous citizen a
tremendous power for good.

Thus the Press for many decades, subsidized
by the traitorous capitalist and under the guise
of a pious mask, catered to the evil designs of
the plutocracy until the gradual awakening of
the people through the independent press at
last understood their hypocrisy.

The independent press, however, attained
its highest degree of efficiency by the establishment of the College of Journalism. Its
foundation slogan, *publicity* on all political and
economic questions, had created a force of
trained journalists—a force "mightier than
the sword" and in a manner far more pene-
trating than the X-ray—pledged to defend the
rights of the citizens. By an educational propaganda it taught the masses how to eradicate
existing evils by the mere exercise of their unalienable right, the ballot box. Indeed in a
government "of the people, for the people and
by the people," resort to force or revolution
was absolutely unnecessary, while these two

most effectual weapons the world had ever
seen, the voting power and the free press, were
at their command.

1921
Balloons and Airships

Strange to say, from the time of Archytas
of Tarantum to Otto Lilienthal, and from
Montgoflier Bros. to Santos Dumont, Bell,
Maxim and Langley, very little or no progress
had been made in practical and safe aerial
navigation.

Though all these inventors, whether cranks
with a smattering of mechanical knowledge,
or veritable savants and scientists, efficient in
physics according to their own accounts, had
studied the subject of aerial flight from the
fowls of the air, the failure of their experiments showed that they were far from grasping
the mysteries of that subtle sagacity and subcon-
sciousness of the birds, by which they balanced
themselves against the currents and velocity
of the winds, and by their intuitive sensitiveness, utilized to the fullest extent their vast
number of muscles and feathers with such
marvelous subtlety.

Like the Italian alchemist in the middle ages, who had constructed the wings of his flying machine with feathers gathered from a dunghill, and who, when attempting to fly, had found himself dumped, by a strange sympathetic affinity, on the very dunghill from which he had gathered the feathers, the efforts likewise, of these illustrious experimenters were crowned by successful failures, by a similar force of attraction, their apparatus either alighting on the branches of trees, or diving into the waters like ducks.

At the beginning of the 20th Century, the consensus of scientific opinion had reached the conclusion, that the successful flying machine of the future would be one, which would be heavier than air and with either a very small balloon or none at all. The various forms of balloons and flying craft, exhibited at the St. Louis exposition became an incentive for renewed efforts by scientists to solve the problem of aerial flight and continued with unremitting zest for nearly a quarter of a century.

It was in the early part of 1919 that the science of aeronautics was radically improved by the discovery of a process for hardening and soldering of Aluminum, by which comparatively light but strong framework and machinery were constructed, and thus gradually the elimination of inflated balloons had become possible.

1922
The Flood in Mississippi Valley

In the spring of this year the Mississippi Valley was flooded and submerged by terrible cloudbursts which, combined with melting of snows on the mountains, and subsequent bursting of dams and levees, devastated a vast area. According to records the lives lost in the inundated districts reached the total of sixty thousand.

1923
Uniform Divorce Laws

The unprecedented increase of divorces all over the United States and the attendant scandalous proceedings at the courts had reached such a maximum, and its baneful influence on the public morals had developed into such a point of danger that, a great awakening among the clergy and lawmakers of the nation was

the result. At a conclave of representatives
of the legal profession from every State in the
Union, was promulgated a uniform divorce
law for the United States of America.

1924

The Zionist Movement
or
The Bursting of the Zion Bubble

The Zionist movement which for thirty years
past gained more than two million converts
and within that period had collected more than
fifteen million dollars, was declared impractic-
able and illusionary !

The estimable originators of this sentiment-
al movement, Herzle, Nordau, Zangwill and
others, although beyond the shadow of a doubt
sincere and well-meaning, through the intensity of their zeal for the amelioration of their
less fortunate brethren, were entirely blindfolded to the intricacies of politics and the
eventful history of the Jewish race, from an
ethnological and psychological point of view.

Some of these true yet misguided philanthropists had passed away and other leaders, less
impressed with the object of the society, had

taken their places. As the Jews are not a pioneer race, the magnanimous scheme of the British government to place them upon a tract of virgin soil at Uganda, in Central Africa, for the purpose of colonization proved chaotic failure, on account of both sociological and economic reasons.

The idea also of establishing a Jewish principality in Palestine, under an absolutely despotic and semi-barbarous government—which butchered her subjects *ad libitum*—was so ridiculous in the extreme, that the questions had become the laughing stock at the political *sanctus sanctorums* of various governments.

In 1923 a tremendous agitation was brought about by the leaders of the opposition, and those in power of the movement were challenged to public debate. The question grew to such proportions that it became a subject for discussion in every orthodox and gentile pulpit. In the press, sociologists, ethnologists and anthropologists took part in the ephemeral arena and analyzed every phase of the subject, relating to the Hebrew race and the Zionist movement, laying bare every fact without reserve.

It was stated by the opposition that though a stream of money had been pouring in from every quarter of the globe year after year, for the cause, no result as yet had been obtained, that great sums had been spent in salaries of the officials and at the dilly-dallying, corrupt courts of the Turkish Sultan.

A learned sociologist likened the Hebrews to a parasitic plant, which derived its existence from the living sap of another. " An Israelite " he declared, " can only exist favorably amongst civilized centres of Christian and gentile communities; that whenever a colony of Hebrews were isolated by themselves, they would inevitably and gradually retrograde, impoverish and at last form a ghetto of misery and squalor."

Another ethnologist of repute expounded the fact, that the Jews were the life and essence of commercial activity and consequently formed an integral part of a prosperous common-wealth. Sublimely industrious, instinctively provident and economical by nature, the Jews were persecuted because of their inherent virtues. He proved by clever historical documents, that their expulsion from Babylon, Egypt, Spain, Russia or wherever their rights were abrogated, were the fundamental causes of the decadence of these countries from which they were expelled.

Others accused the Hebrews of perverting the Golden Rule, of taking advantage of others by their inborn instinct of commercial sagacity, which well nigh approached unscrupulousness and that, being a mere commercial people, their patriotism could well be challenged. Many others advised, however, a propaganda of judicious assimilation of the Israelite with the Christians, contending that the sum total of their virtues and faults was the same as that of their Christian brethren. Meanwhile they advised the Jews that " wherever they lived they ought to make there, their Zions and temples."

After much heated argument and discussion which occupied several days, they at last arrived at the conclusion that the Zionist movement was chimerical! The balance of the funds amounting to many million dollars were voted for the establishment of technical and commercial schools for Israelites and for a fund to aid the judicious emigration of the Jews from ill-favored and congested districts to more favorable localities.

1925-26
The Anglo-American Alliance

The Anglo-American Alliance, by which these two foremost nations of the earth were brought into a happy, fraternal union, and for the achievement of which for nearly a quarter of a century there had been a great effort, in this year had become an accomplished fact!

It was celebrated in a manner unprecedented in the annals of the World's history. Having a profound and far reaching effect, it became an ultimatum for other nations to keep the peace, and goaded them toward the adoption of similar laws, in order to secure the same reciprocal blessings of universal brotherhood.

Much credit was due to that eminent English statesman, now Lord Cunningham, through whose tactful diplomacy this long-sought commercial, social, offensive and defensive alliance became a reality. "I am restrained," said the Professor, looking in the direction of Aurora Cunningham, "to avoid eulogizing him as he justly deserves, for obvious reasons."

At this sentence the students, under the impulse of a sudden admiration, arose to their feet en masse, and, glancing smilingly at Aurora, began rapturously to clap their hands.

This interruption of sympathetic appreciation was brought to a close, by a ringing cry of the Seminary yell: "Dee, Dee, Ya, Ya, Na, Na, Diana.   Hurrah! Hurrah!! Hurrah!!!"

Aurora, blushing deeply, gracefully bowed her acknowledgement and in due form the class was dismissed for the day.

CHAPTER V

The Fistic Duel

THE evening following the moonlight féte, a little after sunset when the western sky, stained with a luminous golden hue, had spread on verdant hills and valleys its radiance of languorous serenity, two motor cyclists were speeding along on a secluded path that led into the main highway, from the Diana Seminary to the West Point Military Academy. The one in advance was wheeling in a leisurely way, while the one behind exerted greater speed, as if in pursuit of the other. He was gaining rapidly so that in a very few minutes the foremost was overtaken, as they both reached a wooden bridge, spanning a small body of water.

Both came suddenly to a stop and dismounted. They were Professor Cielo Allenson and Carlos Don Seville. Don Seville, stung by

the rebuke which the Professor had administered to him the night previous at the Seminary, had decided to take the cowardly course
of waylaying the instructor, in this lonely path,
in order to avenge himself for the righteous
verbal punishment the latter had given him.

Carlos Don Seville was a degenerate scion
of a once noble Spanish family, who had settled in the United States and, like many such
offspring, was engaged in sowing his wild oats.
Financially dependent on a small income, he
was always at his wit's end in order to secure
money with which to continue his reckless
profligacy. Being inherently foolish and im-
provident, he always had the illusion that some
day " something would turn up," and encouraged by this belief he had recourse to gamb-
ling and speculation. As soon as he received
his dwindled allowance, he made himself a
willing prey of card sharps and get-rich-quick
brigands.

Lately, however, he had conceived the idea
of marrying an heiress, and for that purpose
he was hovering about Diana Seminary, annoying the young ladies by his unsolicited atten-
tions, or by brazen audacity intruding uncere-

moniously upon their receptions. His snob-
bish mendacity reached its climax when at the
night of the moonlight soiree he accosted Aurora and Margaret at the intermission of the
dance, while they were sauntering arm-in-arm
along the parterre to a trysting nook.

Notwithstanding Margaret's bold declaration of the previous day, that she wanted to
give the "Jewsky" a piece of her mind, the
feminine temerity and reserve had taken pos-
session of her. The minute they saw him advance they took to their heels, and scampered
back with appealing gestures toward Professor
Allenson who, divining at once the situation,
came gallantly to their rescue, giving Don Seville a scathing reprimand and commanding him
to depart, "unless he desired," announced the
Professor, "to be skinned alive by the war
dogs of the Military Academy."

Don Seville, frightened and abashed, beat an
inglorious retreat and disappeared.

Professor Cielo Allenson, better known at
the Military Academy as the "Old Guard,"
was a venerable man past seventy. He had a
highly intellectual countenance and his silvery
white hair and patriarchal beard gave him

a noble dignity which commanded respect. His strenuous virility and inexhaustible energy was ever a lesson and a rebuke to the many indolent youths who came in contact with him. He was a philosopher of the first rank and an intense lover of nature. Imbued with the deeper knowledge of the subtle workings of natural phenomena, "he could not draw a line," he would say, "between the manifestations of human, animal and vegetable kingdoms."

"Halt you d——d old cur! I demand no apology, but satisfaction," snarled Don Seville abruptly, his face livid with anger.

For a second the Professor was taken aback. But in that very second, through his intuitive and resourceful mind flashed the fact that he was " cornered." He was not a man easily frightened, for as a Major of Volunteers during the Panama and Columbian trouble, and while in his teens, he had led on his handful of men up the hills against the ramparts of the enemy.

But a problem which required instantaneous solution was now presented to him by Carlos Don Seville. It was a problem which neither diplomacy, moral persuasion nor flight of oratory could solve. He realized in that very second that the only way out of this difficulty was to take the coward at his word. It was to be a fistic encounter to the finish.

"Apology, I have none to offer you sir, and am ready to give you such satisfaction as you desire," replied the old man with a dignified firmness.

A remarkable change had taken place in the person of Cielo Allenson. That venerable and spirituelle individual had been transformed in a twinkling of an eye, into a grim and determined looking animal, and like an expert gladiator of the fistic arena, he took the attitude of self-defense.

The "ring" constituted the platform of the wooden bridge, the side rails of which served as the partial ropes. There were no seconds to goad their favorites into action, no referee to decide the doubtful or unlawful blows, no gong to mark the rounds, nor time-keeper to count the defeated out of action. In the languorous glow of the twilight their shadows, reflected in black silhouettes in the placid waters below, were the only silent witnesses of this remarkable encounter.

The contest was constant and in the vernacular of pugilism, superbly game, fast and furious! After the acceptance of the challenge there was no parley between them, but by a sudden rush, Don Seville with his right hand landed a hammering blow on the Professor's skull, which the latter parried with his left with dexterous agility and thus saved a crisis, for if left unchecked the blow would have reached his "solar plexus." In rapid succession the fight continued, Don Seville taking the aggressive and the Professor acting more in self-defense. However, as often as opportunity presented, the latter put in a few well aimed jabs, here and there, on the vital points of Don Seville's anatomy. At the same time it was apparent that Don Seville was getting the best of the contest. The venerable Professor unused to long continued strain of the kind, began to experience difficulty in breathing, and this did not escape Don Seville's observation. Shortly, however, a remarkable change was visible; the Professor seemed to grow stronger with each onslaught he made. He had gained his so-called "second wind" thereby recouping his adroitness and elasticity.

With the consummate skill of a scientific boxer, several times he feigned signs of weakness, by giving false openings, of which his infuriated antagonist attempted to avail himself, thinking the Professor to be on the verge of collapse, only to receive in return several well directed right and left swings on the jaw. These staggered Don Seville to his knees, but he was allowed to rise to his feet by the generous tolerance of the Professor, and the consciousness of this humility caused him to wage the attack with reckless fury. With vulgar oaths he began to resort to foul tactics, trying to hit the defender beyond the limits of decent pugilism.

Don Seville's endurance had now come to its end. His youth, dissipated by debauchery, was undermined of its stability, and in spite of the wide disparity of ages the old man had Don Seville absolutely in his power. It was time, he thought, to terminate these proceedings, so distasteful and undignified to him, but the only way he saw was, to lay aside the tactics of self defense, and adopt those of a punitive retaliation.

With keen alertness he watched for an op-

portunity and when Don Seville, almost crazed
with anger, rushed on him for a clinch, entirely oblivious of the intention of the Professor,
the latter gave a sudden shift to his position
by swinging his body away from his antagonist. Don Seville blindly followed him in his
determination of a desperate onslaught. It
was then that the venerable Allenson shot out
a driving " right upper cut " to the jaw.

This was the finale ! Don Seville staggered
to the rails and toppling over fell with a splash
into the limpid waters below.

The Professor promptly jumped down the
embankment and pulled out his still un-
conscious adversary. If abandoned in that
condition the young man might have drowned
in the shallow waters. The Professor began
to do all in his power to restore him to consciousness; just at that time a farmhand on horseback
appeared on the scene, and by his aid the
Academy ambulance was summoned and Don
Seville was taken to the military hospital.

The Final Blow

CHAPTER VI

Historical Events of the 20th Century
(Concluded)

A SUBDUED applause greeted the Professor the next day when he entered the lecture room to conclude his review of events of the 20th Century. Many floral bouquets were tossed to him by his fair admirers, who were augmented from the other classes, on account of the full detail of his encounter with Don Seville having been spread throughout the Seminary.

The Professor, despite some discoloration on his benign visage, flushed crimson like a bashful child and bowed his acknowledgements, as he began his discourse thus:

1927
Colonization of Central Africa

A system of general colonization on a large scale was, during this year, undertaken by the

British Government. By a new homestead
law, embodying liberal inducements, a vast
army of colonists from all over the British do-
minions were transported to Central Africa.
Thousands upon thousands of persons from the
congested districts of London, Glasgow, Liver-
pool and other large cities, were persuaded to
leave their limited surroundings and uncon-
genial atmosphere, and go to the promising
new land, teeming with boundless opportu-
nities.

Almost the entire inhabitants of the isolated
islands of the Shetlands and Orkneys, who led
an indolent life and eked a meagre existence
by fisheries, joined this grand trek to Central
Africa. Many thousands from the Canadian
provinces and from the United States of America joined this exodus, as did also thousands
from the East Indies. The thorough and ad-
mirable manner in which this laudable movement was handled mitigated the hardships of
transportation, and thus within a few years
more than five million, poor, homeless and
indolent people were given homesteads of
their own, awakening them into energy and
thrift.

Within a decade the population of Central Africa reached the grand total of 25,000,000 industrious, loyal citizens, forming a flourishing dependency, enjoying home rule and liberty, under the protection of British laws and arms.

1928
The Conflagration of the Atlantic Ocean

One of the most wonderful and at the same time awful conflagrations of its kind on record in the history of the world, was that of the apparent burning of the Atlantic Ocean, covering an area one hundred and fifty miles wide. It started in the Gulf of Mexico and, like a prairie fire, only a thousand times more furious, this floating furnace consumed scores of vessels that came into its fiery path.

A few weeks previous to this awful holocaust, the petroleum wells in Texas, New Mexico and Louisiana had run dry, on account of a severe earthquake. It was argued by scientists that, by some subterranean convulsions the oil well fissures had shifted their course, into the waters of the gulf, and the vast accumulation of the inflammable fluid, floating on the ocean had been ignited, either by an electric spark during a thunderstorm, or by some combustible being thrown from a sailing craft.

1929
The Court of Labor

In this year was completed and dedicated the Court of Labor at Washington. This was an imposing building, in which all the momentous labor problems were discussed before a tribunal of disinterested justices, through the able representatives of each faction, without resorting to disastrous strikes, lockouts and disturbances of public comfort.

One of the most remarkable features of this Court of Arbitration was, the colossal group erected between the two grand entrances to the building. This was not a semi-nude female figure with bandaged eyes, holding in her hand the conventional pair of scales, but a Herculean figure of Uncle Sam with his starry hat and glorious chin whiskers, having three faces, three eyes and three arms. Before him were a group of three figures which represented respectively *Capital, Consumer* and *Labor*. In each figure were his eyes wide open and alert, bent with searching scrutiny upon the person in front, to whom he dispensed the just share of each, from a huge cornucopia at his feet.

1930
Landlordism in America

One of the most scandalous evils which had crept gradually in the United States, and eventually became a source of grave anxiety to the government, was a system of Landlordism amongst the very rich. While the general public were slumbering in blissful ignorance, this coterie of avaricious syndicates and multi-millionaires had mysteriously become possessors of vast tracts of lands, in every state of the Union. Some of these holdings comprised hundreds and thousands of square miles in extent.

Miles and miles of shore-fronts, immense areas of forests, whole mountains and lakes, through the conniving, corrupt state and county officials, had passed into the hands of private individuals who, in return had become extremely arrogant in their treatment of the public, by unreasonable restriction.

There seemed to be a mocking sarcasm in the fact when common people sang the National Anthem " America," celebrating its hills and rills, while at every turn of the road, at every shore-front, lake, hill and valley, mountain and forests, the forbidding sign, " No Trespassing Under Penalty," met their eyes, or the repulsive muzzle of the Winchester was thrust into their faces by private watchmen.

This state of affairs had reached such desperate straits, that the public suddenly awakened on the subject. It started first by the protest of the rougher element in the mountain districts, who defied the hired authorities with an organized force. The people committed acts of violence and incendiarism it is true, but by their overt acts they awakened the dormant public to realize the enormity of this scandalous condition of deeding away to millionaires, without the consent of the commonwealth, the common and inalienable heritage of its citizens.

By a unanimous uprising and public mandate the Federal and State authorities were compelled to condemn and confiscate these stolen public lands. New laws were then enacted by which the acquiring of extensive lands was limited, except for agricultural purposes.

1931 ◆

The Discovery of the North Pole

The North Pole, that mysterious geographical locality which for centuries had baffled scientists and explorers, was located and verified by the combined efforts of American and British Governments. The expedition was on a gigantic scale, the force of the explorers being in round numbers two thousand five hundred persons who by a system of depots and rendezvous for supplies, formed almost a continuous chain.

All the latest devices in the form of dynamo-vans and motor-sleds, with balloon attachments were employed in the undertaking. Strange to say the casualties did not exceed more than ten per cent of the expeditionary force. It was discovered, to the great surprise of scientists, that the locality was nothing more than a plateau, studded with cones of ice!

1932

Cure for Laziness

The discovery, by an American, of a germicide for indolence was announced during this year, by which lethargic persons were regenerated into acute activity. It was a concentrated double extract of pitch-blend, containing the radio active element, and when applied to certain parts of the body, it instantaneously transformed the feeling of laziness and ennui, into one of hustling energy and alertness.

The negroes of the Southern States, the natives of tropical countries and also officials in the police departments of large cities, were the ones benefitted by this " golden medical discovery ! "

1933
Capital Punishment

The abolishment of capital punishment in many States of the Union, through the impulsive sentimentality of a minority, had given birth to an old time evil, that of feudalism. It was well for people preaching mercy for murderers, when somebody else was the victim, but when the crime was perpetrated against one of their homes, their feelings were entirely changed. The increase of vendetta was the result, and it occurred with such a lamentable degree of frequency, that the old uncontrovertible Mosaic law, blood for blood, and life for life was re-established.

1934

Abolition of Hereditary Titles in England

The agitation for the abolition of hereditary titles in England caused a crisis in the political and social world of Great Britain. The degeneracy of hereditary nobles, their utter incapacity adequately to fill the positions left by their illustrious ancestors, to the detriment and retrogression of the British government, was the main cause of bringing about this bloodless internecine revolution.

Despite the most strenuous opposition by the friends of the nobles, a new law was added to the revised Magna Charta, by an overwhelming public demand. With few exceptions, it nullified the existing titles, and elevated to peerage only worthy citizens for life, on condition of the good behavior of the incumbent. This excellent law brought fresh and saving blood into the political and civic life of England. The movement precipitated the abandonment of the House of Lords and created in its stead a body called Senatorium, whose members were elected by the tax-paying citizens.

1935
Blowing the Earth Into Fragments

The most remarkable sensation of this year was that of a German scientist and statistician who, after a thorough investigation and mathematical calculation, announced his conclusions, that it was in the range of collective human power, that is, by the combined aid of labor, time, money and high explosives, to rend the earth in twain, or into fragments, and thus create new planets in space, producing new climatic conditions, fauna and life, adaptable to their new positions in the solar system.

1937
An American Penal Colony

The census of this year revealed an unprecedented number of evil-doers, causing great anxiety to the Government. There were recorded ninety-two thousand criminals in prisons and seventy-six thousand paupers in the poor houses. This army of public charges cost the State authorities more than thirty million dollars for their maintenance.

At last by the stress of popular agitation the government adopted a policy of penal colonization. Selecting a desirable island in the Philippines, the Federal authorities succeeded in transporting to the island, within three years, and with half the cost of their maintenance at home, one hundred thousand of these unfortunate malefactors.

Here, they were given every facility and aid, for acquiring and building of homes, farms and factories, and within ten years, under a wise military administration more than half of that number were reclaimed, forming a prosperous and loyal community in the Eastern Hemisphere.

1938
The Great Telescope

With the munificent contributions to a general fund, amounting to two million dollars, by the English, American and French Governments, the greatest telescope which the world has ever known was constructed in Paris. Its lenses measured more than two meters in diameter which, combined with a mammoth revolving camera obscura, brought the moon and some of the planets within the range of visual observation, revealing on Venus and Mars the existence of vegetation and moving objects.

1939
The Earth An Electric Motor

Emil Flammarion, the worthy grandson of the eminent French astronomer, demonstrated by an extremely clever mechanical contrivance in Vacuo, that the Earth was merely an electric Motor in space !

1940
The Trend of Religious Thought

Religious thought or spiritual belief is not an invention of mortals. It is an inborn attribute of the human mind. While man was in his savage or semi-barbarous stage, the ethical and spiritual conceptions were correspondingly crude and religious warfare predominated. With the advance of civilization its development kept pace with it until at the dawn of the twentieth century it had undergone, by natural evolution, a marked metamorphosis.

It gradually divested itself of its legendary mysticism, fantastic dogmas and spectacular schisms, and all intelligent thinkers promulgated a propaganda, not of external forms of worship, but those uncontrovertible basic truths, which always will hold.

It is true that in an era of commercial materialism great masses of people embraced agnosticism and ethical culture, rejecting that supernatural conception of a first cause of which they claimed their limited intellect had a vague idea and was deeper than the hazy human comprehension, yet, the shallow Ingersolian philosophy of attacking a force—which filled millions with hope and goaded them to self-sacrifice, mercy and charity—without substituting something better, was repudiated by the intelligent, and appealed only to the abnormal and the foolish.

This tendency of materialism in religion continued unabated, until the startling announcement of a German scientist — who claimed it was within human power to rend the world in twain—also the marvelous revelation through the mammoth telescope—by which was discovered moving objects and vegetation in other planets—brought on an acute crisis. A tremendous religious revival swept all over the world. It expanded the mental horizon of human conceptions. The existence of living organism in other spheres came within rational deductions. The possible existence of beings far superior in intellect to ourselves, came within the limit of legitimate theorizations, and the more men began to grasp with the co-operation of science, the infinite vastness of the universe, with its numberless millions of habitable worlds, the probability of an intelligent force of vast creative power came within the scope of human understanding.

The forceful passage in the Holy Writ "that God created man in his own image" became more and more lucid. Consequently the pantheism of the old Greeks were revived with more clearness, and the existence of a personal God somewhere in this boundless universe appealed to multitudes with new zest.

"Pray, Professor, what is your opinion of a first cause?" ventured one of the students.

"There are so many mysterious forces," answered the Professor, "that although we cannot see, yet we feel their power and are conscious of their results. And as our mortal organism cannot conceive a thought which is beyond its own limitations, the very idea of our thought of a first cause falls within the range of human conceptions.

When we gaze at an automobile, which is the creation of a creature, we see a wonderful parallelism; its requirements to make it an active energy, bears a strong analogy of its inventor, yet, an automobile with all its requirements for power supplied, is a worthless mass, unless operated and guided by its creator. Does not this vast universe with all its wonderful manifestations suggest a creative force, which governs it ? "

" Albeit, it is not within my province nor in my power to penetrate the veil " continued the Professor, looking up in pensive mood. But as the coral protoplasm begins its edifice from the calcerous mire in the dark recesses of the ocean, upwards through the murky and semi-transparent liquid, finally reaches the pelucid surface, kisses the wave and sees the light, methinks likewise, the spiritual perceptions of mankind which has grown from the depths of savagery and through the maze of intolerance, dogmas and schisms, will go onward in its evolution and perhaps our posterity will at last penetrate the mystic veil and see the light, — God.

1941

The Birthday Anniversary of Noted Centenarians

" Lithia Bingham," " Young Dr. Bray" and "Sister Eddy" received the homage and congratulations of millions of their admirers, on their hundred and fiftieth birthday anniversary.

The remarkable longevity of this trio of Methuselahs was attributed, in the case of the two first mentioned, to their own "cure all" concoctions, and the last, to her scientific revelation of thinking that, there is no such thing as pain or death!

" In closing this review of historical events," said the Professor looking around the auditorium, " there are a few other important happenings that bring us to the present decade.

The remarkable decadence of Germany under a Socialistic regime, a doctrine, that although theoretically seems to be so desirably altruistic, convincing, and in poetry sounds so well, but in practise has proved to be determental to a

life of strenuous efforts, and suicidal to individual ambitions—conditions which are eminent-
ly essential to growing and prosperous communities.

The consequent exodus of Teutons to other
parts of the world that promised freedom to
independent action.

The political union of Spain and Portugal.

The re-conquest by France of Alsace Lorain.

The puerile uprising by a section of Irish
people against England are still fresh in our
memory—and to which most of you have been
eye-witnesses—are some of the events worthy
of record."

Here the Professor, after a pause, changed
his subject to future possibilities and, presenting to the class in eloquent words a glowing,
optimistic picture of conditions for future gen-
erations, brought his discussion to a close.
When he stepped down from the rostrum he
was at once surrounded by the entire class and
was tendered an impromptu but agreeable
reception.

CHAPTER VII

The Regatta

THERE was still one great event before the closing of the academic year of the Diana Seminary Seniors, in which the class had taken extraordinary interest. It was the first time in the history of the Seminary that students were to take part in aquatic sports against male contestants. The day for the great handicap regatta—a four-oared affair—between the Senior class of the Seminary and the Sophomore class of the West Point Military Academy followed directly after graduation,—the class grade being the handicap allowed to the Seminary girls.

Aurora and Margaret, after their avowal and covenant, were again in normal condition, cheerful as of yore, and as they were the most available pair for the aquatic contest, from the beginning they had been chosen unanimously as the exponents of the class of 1960, and they went into the execution of the sport with vim and enthusiasm.

As the event was a unique one, it had become the most lively topic of conversation among the people, and long before it took place had caused widespread interest in the country. Having been advertised and exploited extensively in the daily press, it is needless to say that an unusually large concourse of visitors had arrived by land and water to witness the classic and unusual contest.

The course of the race was laid near Poughkeepsie and was in the shape of a heart, that is, starting at a given point, side by side, they raced about half a mile abreast, then one crew turning to port and the other to starboard, diverging in a parabolic circle, passed each other in the center within a short distance of the starting point, and making counter-circles started on the home run, again abreast. (*See diagram, page 90.*)

The personnel of the Seminary crew consisted of the following young ladies: Aurora Cunningham, coxswain; Margaret MacDonald,

stroke; Horatia Seymour, number one; Eunice
Ward, number two; and Norma Southworth
at the bow.

When the preliminary signal to make ready
was given, both the crews rowed gracefully to

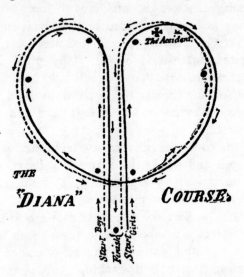

THE
"DIANA"   COURSE.

Start Boys
Finish
Start Girls

The Accident.

the starting ground and began to manoeuvre.
At the sharp report of the signal gun, the two
shells shot past the line almost abreast, amidst
deafening acclamation from the spectators on
the shore and the shrill tooting and whistling

of the sailing craft of every description that had formed almost a compact circle around the course.

The calm and pleasant weather had allowed the waters of the Hudson to run as smooth as a looking-glass, except for the turbulence caused by the ever restless pleasure boats thronged with sightseers, each endeavoring to get a better vantage point of the impending struggle. As the contest progressed, the interest of the watchers began to increase. Thousands of field and marine glasses and lorgnettes were leveled at the racers as they sped along the course.

The teams had now reached the point of divergence, and had begun to recede from each other at every stroke on their parabolic circuit, the boys turning to port and the girls to starboard. But alas! Hardly had the Seminary shell advanced half a dozen strokes when, by some unexpected and inexplicable accident, Margaret's feet slipped off the foot guard and, in an instant, she was thrown into the waters of the Hudson, the shell meanwhile gliding swiftly by.

Instantly the air was filled by a deafening

cry of dismay from the throats of thousands
of eager spectators, coupled with piercing
whistles of the steamboats. What a moment
of anguish for the Diana Seminary girls!
What a shocking sense of humiliation for the
fair contestants! To think that in an event
so crucial for their honor and standing, such
an unforeseen disaster should overwhelm them!

But fate was with them. It was decreed
that such a catastrophe should happen in order
to heighten the grandeur of their ultimate victory. While the spectators were still paralyzed
with the awful situation before them, there
was activity and heroism among the Diana
mermaids in the shell. The instant Aurora
with her alert eyes saw Margaret's mishap,
she realized at once the situation and before
the shell had glided past, she leaned over and
caught Margaret by the hair. By the same
impulsive and almost animal agility, Margaret
grasped Aurora's arm and in another moment,
with less loss of time than would seem possible, she was again in the shell. In a twinkling of an eye the breathless girl had resumed
her place at the oar as if nothing had happened.

Aware of the loss of distance by this un-

On the " Homestretch "

toward accident, which was, in fact, more than
four boats' length, but undismayed and as if
invigorated by her impromptu bath, in order
to recover lost ground Margaret set the pace
at a higher speed and forged ahead with might
and main. When the throngs on land and
water realized what had happened the din of
exultation and cheering was beyond description and this did not abate until the race was
finished. Overwrought by the sight of this
heroic exploit of the girls, men and women
had become madly hysterical. When the shells
crossed each other at the half-mile stake it
was seen that the Seminary girls had recovered
considerable ground, leaving a margin of less
than two boats' length. Encouraged by the
splendid showing made, and goaded to endeav-
or by the rapturous applause of the populace,
Margaret and the rest of the crew seemed to
gain new strength. And when Aurora with
the megaphone gave the order of thirty-six
strokes a minute, they set the pace with marvelous vigor and precision, causing consterna-
tion among their masculine antagonists.

On the completion of the second parabola
of their circuit and when coming on to the

line for the homestretch, it was noticeable that the Seminary shell was only a trifle behind.

The crucial moment had come.

They were now almost abreast on the home-stretch. The intensity of the exciting scene had for a moment cast a profound silence upon the spectators. Every one was straining his eyes and neck to see the momentous finish, only to break again into a bedlam of rapturous shouting when the girls were seen to be in the lead. It was indeed a sight never to be forgotten, when the Seminary shell shot past the finish line a full boat's length ahead, and the girls were acclaimed by the populace as victors.

The intensity of the joy of the throng, and the plight of their utter abandon, can be con-jectured when it was discovered afterwards that eight hundred and ninety-one ladies' and two thousand three hundred and seventy-nine gentlemen's head-gear were picked up in the Hudson. The next day and through the week following, divers reaped a good harvest by bringing up from the river's bed one thousand three hundred and ninety-four field, marine and opera glasses, and two hundred and seven-ty-five lorgnettes, besides innumerable parasols

The Winning Crew

and canes which the people in their abandon
had thrown about.

This episode was the crowning glory of the
Seminary and the beginning of a new epoch
in the history of this institution.

CHAPTER VIII

Dr. Hyder Ben Raaba

LIKE a nebular comet in a far away constellation, so mysterious in its orbit and composition, was Dr. Hyder Ben Raaba, who suddenly made his appearance in the suburbs of the cosmopolitan city of B—— on Long Island. He occupied the spacious mansion of a wealthy merchant, who had abandoned it for a more comfortable lodge in the Adirondacks. Surrounded by somewhat neglected clumps of pines and shrubberies, the establishment was entirely isolated from the highway and most suitable for a man like the Hindoo doctor, who seemed always to desire seclusion.

In order to form an idea of his singular personality, a brief description will perhaps enlighten the reader. He was tall, lank, of swarthy complexion, endowed with a cyranesque proboscis and a moustache which pro-

96

truded like the tusks of a walrus. His eyebrows resembled the moustache in miniature.
His big greenish-yellow eyes, with spacious
white borders and cat-like pupils, were able to
bring to bear an intensely hypnotic gaze, which
had an irresistible and subjective power. As
he was invariably attired in the picturesque
costume of his country, and from the fine texture of the silken turban and embroidered
robes, could easily be conjectured that he belonged to a high caste and noble Hindoo family. He had a peculiar walk, continually
swerving from side to side as he moved, wriggling and swinging his indispensable jessamine
cane, which from its serpentine convolutions
looked as if it had been hardened while in
convulsions.

The people of the neighborhood, although
amused by his strange antics, entertained great
respect for him. To some, especially to young
people, he seemed a monstrosity. They had
already nick-named him the "Crazy Doctor."
Vague rumors circulated among the gossip-
loving residents that he was a political refugee,
who, finding his life in danger in India, had
fled from his native land. But no one doubt-

ed his ability as a physician and surgeon, for in a short time he had founded a reputation that commanded respect.

His cadaverous look, his strange hypnotic eye and mysteriously eccentric movements, enhanced a hundredfold his reputation rather than damaged it. Every one considered him a man of great learning, a wizard in the science of healing and stood aghast exclaiming wonderingly, "Whence cometh this mighty healing power?"

When Dr. Ben Raaba made his advent in B—— he was accompanied by a robust, well-formed and intelligent-looking Levantine Jew servant, Esau by name. This person minded his own business, and proved himself to be a very discreet servant, never divulging his master's secrets to any outsider. A few months after taking up their residence, however, the place resembled a private menagerie. Scores of cats, dogs, of high and low degree, pigs and goats of every size made their appearance.

Dr. Hyder, notwithstanding various opinions of others, was in reality a mysterious and remarkable man; despite his thorough British education and extensive travels in foreign lands, was a believer in the tenets of a Hindoo sect called the Saktian Yogis, a believer of Mahadeva, whose spouse of a dual nature—spiritual and material principles in one—has three qualities : first, Dominion and Desire ; second, Rectitude and Wisdom, with power to control senses ; and third, Violence and Passion.

The Doctor, moreover, was conversant with all the Hindoo mysticism and sciences, astronomy and magic. He was capable of restraining respiration, besides being a natural born hypnotist of great power. Modern practical medicine and surgery were also among the Doctor's accomplishments, as he had a seven year course in the National University of Medicine of London.

His appearances in public began to diminish gradually after the various animals were received there, as he was engrossed in his laboratory, engaged in some experiment in vivisection ! Indeed, in the dead of night, weird and uncanny sounds often emanated from the inner recesses of his laboratory. Sometimes a piteous mew, or the piercing caterwaul of felines, or the whining of dogs. At other times, the plaintive beating of a goat, the squeaking of a goose or the squeal of a pig broke the silence of the night, while at intervals, now and then, several owls on the roof gave vent to their weird hootings.

This state of affairs naturally gave an awful aspect to the place, and kept the inquisitive villagers at a distance, while the mischievous youngsters gave the place no trouble from trespassing. The only incident which reached the public was told by a precocious youth who, with grim determination, strived to unravel the mysteries of the place, on a cloudy night had crawled into the garden, climbed a tree, and hidden himself until later on, when the full moon appeared above the horizon and cast its hazy light through the clouds. Then an uncanny sight was unfurled before his eyes; there, sitting under the shadow of a weeping willow tree, the Hindoo Doctor, apparently, was in the act of hypnotizing a goat, with weird gestures and incantations. Unnerved by this strange sight, the intruder, losing his grip and footing, fell to the ground. The hooting of an owl and a fiendish howl from the Doctor gave the youth a further impetus

Hyder Ben Raaba and the Goat in the Garden

to scamper for life, over shrubberies and picket
fence, out of the domain of the Hindoo vam-
pire !

Upon the youth's recital of his experience,
the feeling of mystery and fear increased among
the unsophisticated people of the neighborhood and they kept shy of the place.   But the
climax of their apprehension was reached when,
shortly after, the following curious sign adorned
the main gate to the house :

```
x ...........................  ..............x
:                                            :
:        DR. HYDER BEN RAABA                 :
:                                            :
:   VIVISECTIONIST AND RE-INCARNATOR         :
x..........................  ....  ...........x
```

What was the meaning of these significant
words on his shingle, "Vivisectionist and Re-
incarnator?" What was the mission of this
mysterious man? To what line of surgical
science did this assortment of animals contribute, whose piteous wails ever and anon emanated from his laboratory?   Up to that time a
chain of wonderful discoveries and marvelous
achievements had been attained by profound
savants in surgical and pathological subjects :

The creation of life germ cells: The trepanning of skulls and the re-arrangement of the brains: The grafting of skin, nose and ear: The infusion of new blood: The pre-natal determination of sexes: The separation of mind from the body, by subjecting persons in a cataleptic state by hypnotism: And last but not least, the hibernation for an indefinite period of living bodies by suspended animation.

These amazing triumphs, each more startling than the other, were the records of past achievements.

Could there be anything more astounding?

Even so, Dr. Hyder Ben Raaba, who was conservant with all the above mentioned exploits of experimenters, had conceived one of the boldest and extraordinarily audacious of surgical feats, the successful demonstration of which would startle the world and make men stand aghast with wonder. In fact, by the display of his professional sign, it was a foregone conclusion that he had succeeded in his experiments.

By the aid of science, occultism and wonderful magic, he had transformed the sexes!

CHAPTER IX

A Ray of Hope

IT was the day of departure of Aurora Cunningham for London, England. Margaret had accompanied her in an automobile to the city of B—— to see her off. Their parting had an unusual sadness as they stood on the deck of the Dynamoship " Columbia "—a four-day ocean greyhound. They seemed to be paralyzed at the barrenness of the future, looking into each other's eyes as if trying to challenge sincerity to their oath of allegiance.

It was extremely touching indeed, when they were compelled by the officers of the ship to take their final leave, and as the Columbia began to recede gradually from its moorings, her prow compassed to the British Isles, Aurora's lithe figure could be seen at the stern of the boat, throwing kisses and waving her handkerchief toward Margaret, until the distance grew wider and farther and the figure fainter and at last was lost to view.

Left alone on the shore, Margaret did her utmost to control her emotions of parting from her beloved friend. With suppressed feelings she mounted her automobile reluctantly, and bade the chauffeur proceed to New York City, from whence, after a short repose, she intended to take the train for her home in Wyoming.

She had hardly gone a mile or two out of the city of B—— when her emotions had swelled beyond her capacity of control and she became delirious in her seat in the auto. Some pedestrians by the way, noticing that something unusual had happened to the fair occupant, called the attention of the chauffeur to his charge. He brought the machine to a standstill and the necessity of enlisting the services of a doctor was at once apparent.

One of the bystanders suggested that the nearest available doctor was tho Hindoo surgeon, Dr. Hyder Ben Raaba, about a furlong farther down the road, and thither the patient was wheeled with all possible haste, and within a few minutes she was in the Doctor's reception room.

After a cursory examination Ben Raaba appeared somewhat puzzled. " She is in a state of coma," he said, rubbing his forehead with his bony fingers, "but I do not yet see any physical cause to induce that condition. It seems to me," he added, " that every function of the organs are in a perfectly normal state."

His face brightened at once, however, with a smile of victory. A happy thought had come to his fertile mind. He had thought of the singular methods practised by the diagnostician Avicene of Balk—the father of occult Diagnosis—and the words of the Cashmerian poet came to his memory, who nearly ten centuries previously had said: " The pulse of the loving, beats higher, agitated only at the name of the beloved."

Taking thereupon her pulse into his hand, he began to question the chauffeur, where she had gone, with whom, what was the other young lady's name, etc. He knew that, although she was in a state of coma, her senses of hearing and of understanding were performing their regular functions. At the mention of the name of Aurora Cunningham there

was a remarkable change in Margaret; her
pulse began to beat double quick!

After repeating the experiment, and satisfy-
ing himself that the cause was a matter pertaining the heart, in fact the girl's infatuation
for her departed friend, and that there was
nothing in the Materia Medica as an antidote,
that the only restorative remedy that could be
found was in hypnotic occultism, he leaned
over the prostrate figure before him and whis-
pered some words into her ear.

The correctness of his diagnosis became
plainly evident.   The patient, with perfect
tranquility, opened her eyes, and with a com-
placent smile looked into the face of her re-
storer.   After a few more magnetic passes and
words of encouragement from the Wizard, she
had completely recovered herself, to the amazement of the anxious group of persons who had
gathered there, curious to know the fate of the
fair occupant of the automobile.   Within half
an hour she again entered her auto and proceeded on her way to the city.

The new and remarkable personality of
Hyder Ben Raaba, however, left an ineradica-
ble impression upon her mind, so much as at

times to divert her thoughts from dwelling
upon Aurora and concentrate upon the strange
visage of Hyder Ben Raaba. After a repose
of a few days in New York, having made all
the preparations for the intended journey, she
left the metropolis and arrived in due time at
her paternal home in Wyoming.

Hardly a month had elapsed after her return
when there was another crisis in her life. Her
father was taken suddenly ill and died, and
she was left an heiress to a large fortune con-
sisting principally of lands, mines and cattle.
Being without any relatives to guide her, Margaret was compelled to settle matters for herself, and daily she was confronted by hundreds
of annoying details. These consisted of many
entangling affairs of her lamented father, who
had left her sole legatee, prospective aspirants
who sought her hand in marriage, her solemn
and binding oath to Aurora, and, strange as it
may seem, the grotesquely hideous face of Ben
Raaba began to flit before her mind's eye, perplexing and haunting her incessantly.

One evening when she was thus absorbed
in deep meditation, the postman brought her
a letter. It was mailed from B——. Excit-

edly she tore open the envelope and from it fell the professional card of Dr. Hyder Ben Raaba. The same weird and ominous words were printed under his name: " The Vivisectionist and Re-incarnator " ! On the other side were scribbled a few lines, making inquiry about the state of her health.

The card, ah ! the strange and significant words, vivisection and re-incarnation began to assume a deep meaning. She placed the card tremblingly upon the table and fell into a profound study. Her quivering frame, the rise and fall of her heaving breast and the change of color of her face alternatively from pallor to a feverish flush, indicated that there was a revolution going on within her immaculate bosom.

At last she seemed to come to some determination; tremblingly she grasped a pen and wrote a letter to Ben Raaba, the contents of which never became known to any but herself and the Hindoo doctor. Within a fortnight she received an answer which seemed to satisfy her.

Within two months she had managed hastily to dispose of all her personal property and real estate without any reserve, and then she disappeared from her Western home and sur-roundings and was lost forever to her former friends.

CHAPTER X

The Transformation

IT was near the end of September. The seaside resorts on Long Island were deserted by the gay health-seekers from the adjacent cities, and the inhabitants of the villages along the South Shore, from Rockaway to Montauk, had dwindled to their normal number of rural residents except the city of B——— which, on account of its shipping interests, still retained a lively activity.

The day was dismal and damp, foreboding a rainy spell. There were scarcely any people on the streets and at dusk, when the Montauk express stopped at the station of B———, there were only a few passengers to alight.

One of them was a young woman attired in black, with a thick veil of similar hue drawn over her face. She looked furtively up and down the platform with painful anxiety, and

espying an automobile a few rods below the
station, walked toward it hesitatingly, at the
same time pulling from her wrist-bag a crimson handkerchief. The chauffeur on the machine seemed to understand the meaning of
the signal, for at once jumping down he advanced to meet the stranger.

After several words were exchanged in subdued tones, he escorted the veiled lady to the
vehicle and in a few minutes they were speeding down the road toward the Hindoo doctor's
sanitarium. The woman, of course, was Margaret MacDonald and the chauffeur none other
than the Levantine Jew, Esau, the Doctor's
discreet servant. When they arrived at Ben
Raaba's domicile it was almost pitch dark, and
not a soul could be seen in the vicinity. At
the ringing of the door-bell, Ben Raaba himself appeared and sedately welcomed Margaret,
conducting her into the reception room.

Shortly after, when Esau had withdrawn,
they were sitting *tete-a-tete* at a table, perusing some mysterious documents to which at
last, Margaret, taking a pen, subscribed her
signature.

The documents were nothing else than the

legal contract, which Margaret had signed, offering herself a willing subject to undergo a
mental and physical metamorphosis, and ab-
solving Ben Raaba from any responsibility if the
experiment should prove unsuccessful or fatal!

After a fortnight of dietary preparation, Margaret was taken into the Laboratory of the
Wizard and immediately hypnotized by him
into a state of cataleptic coma.

An awful sensation crept over one upon
looking around about this den called the Laboratory. Glittering saws and scalpels were
hung in rows on the walls; lances, beakers and
retorts were scattered on the tables and on the
floor, and a hundred and one other apparatus
and bottles could be seen upon the shelves.

A big cat-owl perched on a pedestal in one
corner, and a black tom-cat with intense
green eyes, prowling about the room, gave to
the scene a cabalistic and weird aspect. Here
among these uncanny surroundings Dr. Hyder
Ben Raaba isolated and busied himself with
continuous vigilance for many months in order
to achieve an undertaking that seemed miraculous and impossible.

*   *   *   *

Ben Raaba's Laboratory

Through the lapse of so many long and tedious months Dr. Hyder Ben Raaba had come to the completion of his assiduous labors,—labors which had almost exhausted his consummate skill in hypnotism, surgery and magic.

After a final but scrupulously careful examination of the patient, assuring himself that every muscle, nerve, gland and artery were in their proper places, he paused a moment before the prostrate body. It was a solemn and tragic moment. Signs of intense anxiety were visible upon his otherwise imperturbable visage, betraying the fact that he was in a crucial predicament.

What, if on awakening the patient, he found her a maniac irrevocably bereft of reason? What, if his re-incarnated subject should prove to be a hideous Frankenstein or a monstrosity devoid of finer senses? What, if she should prove to be a man with effeminate mind and manners?

Such and a thousand other similar fears and misgivings were flashing in that moment through his mind, but at last, confident of his ultimate success, and undaunted with apprehensions, he assumed a determined countenance and commenced to undo the hypnotic spell, in order to restore his subject to life and energy.

With eyes dilated, eyebrows knit, and arms stretched—holding in one hand a magic wand —this future Mephisto uttered some mysterious words in sepulchral intonations, snapped his fingers three times, and presto !

The spell was broken !

The full magical effect of his audacious undertaking was evident, for scarcely had the last syllable of those mysterious and incomprehensible words left his shriveled lips, when a sudden tremor shook the frame of Margaret and, with a subdued groan, indicative more of a sensation of bliss than of pain, she opened her eyes.

A triumphant smile pervaded her countenance, as if awakening from an Utopian dream. Dr. Ben Raaba, meanwhile perceiving the crowning success of his work, and standing beside her, began to exclaim with rapturous joy, " Metempsychosis ! Metempsychosis ! "

The patient at once became conscious that her bodily transformation was complete, for it did not take her long to realize it as HE stood there, a beautiful specimen of manhood !

This miraculous transformation brought to light another remarkable mental discovery. It was discovered by the Doctor that all the accomplishments, knowledge and mental attributes possessed by Margaret, prior to her re-incarnation, had been intensified a hundredfold in their entity into those of aggressive, daring and strenuous masculinity.

Margaret, assuming forthwith a masculine name, remained a few months under the care and tutelage of Ben Raaba, in order to acquire further important knowledge in hypnotism, diplomacy, etc., that would be of invaluable service in his future career, and it was not until September, almost one year after the advent of the patient, that he reluctantly bade good-bye to Hyder Ben Raaba, and was again lost in the vortex of humanity.

CHAPTER XI

Lord Cunningham, Viceroy of India

HARDLY had Margaret reached her home in Wyoming, when Aurora likewise was welcomed by her people in England. Her father, whose brilliant career upward from the ranks of the common people had astonished the diplomats of the world, meanwhile had been raised to the highest rank of peerage.

Being a born leader of such inexhaustible sagacity and acumen, his promotion from one important position to another was not only inevitable but necessary, and hardly a month had elapsed since Aurora's return to London, before he was gazetted as Lord Cunningham, Viceroy to India.

The situation at that time in India was quite a delicate one, on account of the Thibetan boundary question with Russia. The latter had raised her periodical spasm of aggression, in order to attain certain political ends at home, and the departure of Lord Cunningham was therefore hastened.

It was near the end of November when Lord Cunningham, his wife and beautiful daughter were regally received in Bombay. Distinguished looking in his six feet two inches of height, with a leonine countenance, The Lord at once captivated the Indian rajahs, princes, and also commanded the respect of the populace. His courteous manners, forceful and firm proclamations and actual philanthropic undertakings coupled with his propaganda of dispensing equal justice to all, aroused at once the enthusiasm, patriotism and loyalty of every class, and quieted the racial differences and political disquietude among the people.

The Russian government, seeing this solid phalanx of unity and change of sentiment of the Indian people, beat a hasty retreat under the subterfuge of quelling an alleged disturbance on the borders of Manchuria.

In order to give himself an opportunity for a general introduction, Lord Cunningham decided to hold a reception and dance. It was planned to follow the style of entertaining then in vogue, a combination of literary and musical talent to be followed by a reception. Among the many who had consented to contribute to the evening's entertainment, and occupying the place of honor, was the celebrated savant Abou Shimshek, the Astronomer of Ispahan, who had just returned from an adventurous expedition to the Himalayas to investigate Nature's wonders.

Lord Cunningham being aware of the presence of the celebrated prodigies, the Dusky Quartette, who were on their itinerary to Bombay, had sought and engaged their services for the occasion. An American violin virtuoso, Spencer Hamilton, who had created a furore in Simla a week previously at a fashionable society recital and was acclaimed as an unequaled maestro of his instrument, had also promised to appear during the entertainment and render a few selections on the violin.

On the night of the Soiree a great multitude of natives as well as eminent European personages were present, in all the picturesque splendor of the habilaments of their respective countries. There were Maharajahs, dazzling with diamonds, accompanied by their retinue blazing with silver and gold embroidered costumes, Ascetic Brahmins and sombre looking Fakirs from the seats of learning of Hyderabad, mysterious emissaries from the sacred city of Delhi, learned Sheiks with flowing patriarchal beards from Arabia and Egypt, Magicians from all over Persia, besides all fashionable folk from military posts throughout the East Indian Empire.

Dashing and handsome officers vied with each other in their endeavor to do homage to the beautiful Aurora, who was enthroned next to her mother. After a prelude on the dulciphone, Abou Shimshek, amidst the huzzah and clamor of the assemblage, with great dignity came forward, and with uplifted arms, invoking the spirits of Hafiz and Firdozy to endow him with eloquence, began the account of his thrilling adventure as follows:

CHAPTER XII

Adventures of Abou Shimshek, the Astronomer of Ispahan

"UP, on the Kinchinginga's lofty summit, where earth and heavens meet, where myriads of crystalline, icy temples in their immaculate and prismatic garbs here and there, and manywhere abound, temples, in whose solid glacial niches saints perpetually hold communion with Mahatma's Son.

"I said, I was upon the Kinchinginga's. Aye, for no other purpose than on a mission sublime, to climb nearer to heaven in search of the Creator's secrets profound and reveal them to the human race. Day after day, thus, dauntless and resolute, I scaled craggy precipices. Through mammoth caverns of desolate solitude I wended my way up to reach the goal of my ambition, lured there by my faith.

"Night after night, thus, I gazed and

Abou Shimshek in the Cave

scanned heaven's canopy, studded with twinkling jewels.   But alas! it seemed, farther and
more remote grew the space between me and
the blue heaven, with no mortal kind to cheer
my solitude, except the wails of hungry jack-
als and the wild groans of the Bengal tiger
fierce, with myriads of phantom spirits, darting here and there, in weird, fantastic forms;
I could not tell whether they were the creatures of some world unseen, or the ghosts of
Gothama and his saints keeping vigil over the
faithful.   But at last, so dire and awful did
grow my solitude that, overcome by fright and
fatigue, I retreated into a glacial cave beneath
a lofty peak.

"I laid my head on a chilled stalagmite, the
frozen floor to my back, and my face and belly
against what I thought to be the dome of my
cavern.   But, by the sacred wart that grew on
Gehangire's nose, what reality!   What a wonderful sight!   A new world, revolving through
space—entirely different from ours as it had
living souls and vegetation in a far more advanced stage of develoment than ours,—was
revealed to my astonished eyes!

" The greatest efforts of men are brought to

naught with the elements controlled by Allah's command, or are so small in scale and scope as to be beyond compare with His wondrous works. Through the greatest telescope that man's ingenuity and skill can produce, astronomers cannot agree whether the canals of Mars are single or double.

"Pshaw! Away with those numberless imposters who have deluded mankind with their consummate lies! Some even claim to have traversed the inter-etherial space by flying machines, whose construction was revealed to them in a "sealed package" or found in boxes, buried in tombs and mummies of days gone by! The marvelous medium through which I saw this celestial panorama was nothing strange; the cavern into which I so unconsciously was led was an observatory by nature made!

"Its dome was a mammoth telescope, composed of lenses of great magnitude, various in size and shape. Lenses made of purest water, distilled by the thundering clouds and filtered through heaven's ether. Lenses congealed by the zephyrs that gently blow from Mount Everest's snow-capped brow; lenses, annealed and polished through centuries by the fiery orb that governs our earth, from its moorings in wondrous space. Here, to my eye, was a telescope most complete. It brought that strange planet so near as to make me inhale its very atmosphere, touch its soil and waters with my outstretched arms. And which, with your kind tolerance, I will briefly relate.

" The first element on this marvelous world, which my attention did attract, was the wonderful hues of its firmament. There were no " inter-luminous rays " of " rosy radiance " nor " amber isles " floating over " golden seas " of sunsets, or similar trash, that our poets here below have sung for ages gone, over and over again. But instead, wonderfully colored panels of exquisite designs, the whole changing as if by a dissolving slide, at every atmospheric vibration, into still more beautiful patterns, a veritable Kaleidoscope !

"On consulting my astronomical calculations I found that this strange phenomenon was caused by the peculiar inclination and ascension of this planet toward the sun ! As I was scanning this sublime panorama, with rapturous admiration, my attention was diverted to an expanse of water. Its constantly foaming and sparkling nature induced me to examine it more closely and, to my great surprise, upon analysis I found it to be similar to delicious cream soda, with cakes of ice floating on it, and the whole impregnated with phosphates— on account of the immense guano deposits left by extinct birds, along its shores !

"But my surprise was still increased when, turning my eyes toward land, I beheld numerous geysers and fountains, spouting up streams and sprays of waters of various hues. I tasted them one by one and, to my delight, I found some of them to be composed of seltzero-caffein, some of bromo-cocain, some others containing an infusion of Cerebrine. But one of the most peculiar fountains which I discovered was one that had a zig-zag motion and luminous color.

"On partaking of a sip of it, I suddenly experienced a strange sensation going through my body, exhilarating and rejuvenating my whole system, eradicating all the dandruff from my scalp, purifying my blood and dispelling at once that "tired feeling." I gave to this fountain the name "Electrolinaris" on account of the large percentage of " the electric fluid " it contained!

"The vegetation that grew on this marvelous planet, although analogous to our terrestrial trees and herbs—having roots, trunks and branches—was entirely of different order. These forms were a combination of vegetable and animal kingdoms, because of their construction and sensitiveness. I noticed, for example, trees whose leaves changed color several times a day, some others which emitted extraordinary sounds, while still others shrank and expanded instantaneously.

"But their fruits were still more curious. Of course to satisfy my natural curiosity, I picked and tasted many of them. They were nothing but our manufactured confections. Still how delicious they were! Here was a tree the folds of whose musical leaves shielded delicious chocolates, there another tree whose branches dropped ripe and luscious glace bon-bons of various flavors, while sugar-coated violets and jasmines abounded promiscuously on perfuming bushes.

"During my inspection I came across a palm-like plant full of innumerable shining objects which, on closer scrutiny, to my amazement I found to be miniature incandescent radium lights of great brilliancy.

"As I proceeded with my investigations I saw another plant whose branches were studded with brilliant scintillating globules. I hastened to examine them and they were neither more nor less than veritable crystals of diamonds. Now it is well known that the diamond consists of pure carbon in crystalized form. This plant had simply the power of absorbing pure carbon by its roots, and passing through its wonderfully peculiar fibres exuded and condensed them on its branches like gumdrops, where they were hardened by the action of its equally strange atmosphere. I have on my person—as you will observe—a few specimens which I picked at random.

"And now in reference to animals. Perhaps you will expect me to describe to you strange megalotheruses of immense proportions, or gigantic mammalian quadrupeds, mammoth flying dragons, serpents and birds, but herein I must disappoint you. The truth is, although I searched diligently for such paleozoic monsters, I came in contact with none. Surprised

as I was myself, it explained itself on my discovering an ampitheatre-like enclosure wherein
were stored, in great numbers, the lifeless
skeletons of unimaginable beasts which had
existed on this planet in centuries past. And
as on our earth the large animals are gradually becoming extinct on account of the advance
of civilization, with the exception of the Tammany Tiger, the American Eagle and the
British Lion, I came to the conclusion that on
this new sphere likewise, because of its far
advanced stage of civilization, they were already extinct.

"I could not, however, suppress my laughter
on seeing in this collection of monstrous wild
beasts, two specimens of two-legged mammalians or human beings. I speedily came to the
conclusion that they were either some of those
blatant fools, who had ventured on journeys
to remote planets in their flying machines, or
some of our ultra-civilized English and American pioneers, gone on missions of "grab" and
"benevolent assimilation!"

"Anon, I come to the most interesting stage
of my adventure, that of seeing the most intelligent animals of this new planet, which it

seemed had full control over it, so that there remained no doubt in my mind of their being the human race of this strange world. Consequently, I watched them closely, and verily I found them to be far more advanced in civilization and bodily construction than we, mankind. They were so constructed that they had all the advantages which we are obliged to supply ourselves by artificial means and devices. As I describe them, you will, to a certain degree, form an idea of how they looked.

"They had only one eye on the top of their heads, a large globular organ, however, having like the dragon fly a multiform lens. This eye was shielded by an umbrella-shaped substance of a hard bony nature. Thus protected they could see all round about them at the same time, or whichever side they wanted, without inconveniencing themselves by craning their necks.

"I thought it would have been a great blessing if we mortals here possessed such optics. Think of the advantage while going about in a crowded thoroughfare of a great city, to see where you are stepping, to read the various newspaper bulletins, to watch the clock on the spire, to recognize your friends in the surging throng and besides all these to be able to dodge adroitly the numerous trolley cars and auto-mobiles at the same time !

" In place of the eyes, there were two large circles, covered by a delicate membrane of great sensitiveness, which instead of sight was used for speech, because they did not speak with their mouths and in audible sounds, but with these two curious circles they carried on a conversation in " silent eloquence," instanta-neously transmitting their thoughts to each other, a veritable telepathic medium, as it were !

" Their noses and mouths were likewise equally strange and entirely different from ours in construction, although to all appear-ances they had the same form and occupied similiar places. For instance, they could ex-tend their nostrils at pleasure, shut air-tight or open at will, so that at the mere suspicion of a bad odor they could instantly elongate their proboscis to some point at which pure air and perfume abounded.

" The mouth was so constructed that they could expand and contract it like a chameleon's,

but about three or four yards, and in such in-
conceivable velocity that its rapidity of action
was beyond calculation. Its usefulness was
manifold, because they not only took nutrition
by it, but it was also a very formidable weapon
of attack and defense.

" They wore absolutely no clothing, consequently were annoyed by no tailor-made suits,
no bloomers, no furbelows, but nature itself
had provided with all that was desirable.
Their skins were covered from the neck to the
shoulder with white swansdown, and from the
shoulders to the waist with a fine silky fur,
resembling in color and texture the best quality of seal-skins, while from the waist sprout-
ed all around the loveliest crop of hanging
ostrich feathers. There was no difference in
male and female attire. As women nowadays
are speaking of equal rights, and are adopting
masculine tendencies, I believe we are on the
right line of advancement to reach the same
destination.

" Their manner of locomotion was another
surprise to me as I watched them darting deft-
ly here and there. Upon examination of their
lower extremities, I found it to be simply loco-

motion by electricity. Under their feet were several wheels of natural formation and which- ever direction they wanted to go, they set the locomotive current to any degree of celerity. Think of it! Each person having his own automatic rapid transit!

"As I became intensely interested in those strange beings, I felt curious to know and study their social manners and discover whether they experienced any emotions, sorrows or mirth. Consequently I changed my observa- tions to these particulars. In searching through the gardens and flowery bowers that abounded in a certain locality, it was not necessary for me to wait very long. My eyes rested upon a comical spectacle, which left no doubt in my mind that it was a case of amorous depreda- tion. It was simply, as I judged, an act of stealing kisses. Oh, the rascal! Here was a maiden sweet and fair, overcome perhaps by fatigue, lying on the velvety grass of cobalt blue, her head resting on a natural eiderdown- topped toadstool, and there, a precocious youth, perched on a branch of a tree above, his elastic mouth in close contact to that of the maiden, busily gathering, like the hummingbird, the nectars of osculatory bliss, while his globular eye kept watch round about for any uncere- monious or hostile intruder!

" In vain I tried to imitate.   Ah ! I still feel the thrill.   In fact, I would not object to have a mouth so formed, even in this vain world of ours.   I believe there are flowers here also, ever in bloom, like the fairy maiden above.

" In reference to the pleasures and enjoy- ments of these marvelous beings, I was some- what nonplussed to find that there were no theatres or places of amusement.   The fact was that in every respect they were very, very practical.

" When they wanted to laugh, they simply went to certain valleys in their locality where, on inhaling its atmosphere, they became al- most hysterical in their ecstasy of joy, giggling, ha-haing and continuing in such hilarious laughter without stop until they were thor- oughly satisfied.

" I became curious to know the nature of this atmospheric element which produced such merriment, and on careful analysis found the air to be strongly impregnated with pure nitrous oxide or " laughing gas," an inferior quality of which was formerly used by our dentists.

"Likewise, when they felt a desire to cry, they went to another neighborhood, where certain bushes abounded, bearing on their drooping branches a profusion of " Job's Tears," the sight of which so affected the visitors that they were at once transformed into veritable Niobes—all tears. They wept, sighed and wailed until their longing had subsided.

"Their solution of the habitation problem was, I think, that which wise men on this earth have been trying to solve from the beginning of creation. This Utopian planet contained no dwellings built by mankind, consequently there were no taxes, no new land theories, no internal revenue or protection embargoes. The planet itself produced everything without the aid of its people and they enjoyed the fruit of the soil equally.

"Whenever these creatures desired to rest, they retired to certain localities, where millions of velvety couches grew like toadstools, on which they reclined, while the vegetation around, with its narcotic perfumes, lulled them quietly to sleep. .

"The duration of their day, which was a continual twilight of variegated designs, was according to my chronometer fifty hours long, and they divided it into two equal parts, twenty-five hours of which they slept in balmy dreamlands, while the other twenty-five they indulged in all kinds of recreations and no work at all! Ah! as the working hours of our laboring classes are decreasing day by day by the glorious medium of Unionism, I am happy to predict that we are on the right path of some day reaching that millenium of doing nothing, so that we shall at last have twelve hours of sleep, and twelve hours of recreation!

"When I saw all these wonderful things, I confess, I forgot my mission sublime, and determined then and there to transport myself to that celestial sphere. Consequently I approached one of them and appealed for admission to that land of rest and perpetual bliss. Scarcely had I spoken when I felt the atmosphere about me become suffocating; there was thunder and lightning and a sepulchral voice was heard to say:

"No earthly domination here."

This dread injunction rendered me insensible and when consciousness returned I found myself at the foot of the Kinchinginga's, amidst the ruins of that wonderful telescope by nature made ! "

CHAPTER XIII

Spencer Hamilton

THUNDEROUS applause of appreciation greeted Abou Shimshek, at the conclusion of his interesting recital, and bowing right and left his acknowledgements, with beaming countenance he retired to his seat.

An intermezzo of mellifluent music in the interim was followed by the celebrated " Dusky Quartette." This aggregation consisted of the following members: Madam Celeste D'oumbalooloo, a south African soprano of heavenly sweetness, and a beauty of "hippopotamic gracefulness ;" Miss Guza Mulomba, the Kaffir prodigy, with a contralto voice of tremulous colorature; Signor Bombasto Reales, of Kabaloogan, a Philippino tenor of high pitch and clearness, and the basso, Signor Dido Abazuza, a Maori celebrity of thunderous profundity.

"The Dusky Quartette"

Indeed, under the felicitous protection of British and American sovereignty, these colonies had made such rapid advancement toward civilization, that they had produced an abundance of men and women of extraordinary talent and capacity in art and music, so as to eclipse their confreres of Huugarian and Polish origin, in days gone by.

The portfolio of their operatic creations was a revelation. Especially did an operatta, called "Phantasie Senegambienne" arouse the enthusiasm of the audience to such a high pitch of spirituelle tension that at the conclusion—regardless of the (color line)—there was a simultaneous rush of both sexes to where the singers stood. A scene of indescribable osculatory battle raged, the sound of the contact of those luscious thick lips of the Dusky Quartette echoing and reverberating to the utmost recesses of the spacious hall. It took quite a long time before this charming labial fusillade of musical appreciation subsided.

After another soothing interlude, giving the assemblage a chance to recover their composure, a clamorous applause brought forth the American violinist, to make his first debut in

Bombay. As he stepped forward, Spencer Hamilton instantly made a deep impression upon the audience. His masterful technique and wonderful skill of execution, when he rendered a new composition of his own, called " The Niagara," aroused anew the enthusiasm of the throng and, under pressure of vociferous acclamation, he was obliged to render another selection.

With the appearance of this splendid young specimen of manhood upon the platform there was created in the bosom of Aurora a strange psychological condition. Although surrounded with many gallant officers and youths of noble lineage, she was perceptibly affected by the sight of this handsome young American musician. At a glance at the violinist there sprang in her heart afresh the memories of her college days in America.

A sudden sense of sadness swept over her, and her infatuation for her chum Margaret, and the recollection of their solemn vows, flashed vividly through her perplexed brain, evoking several deep sighs from the depths of her constant heart. Notwithstanding the cringing advances of many officers of position and wealth, as well as scions of nobles, she had fallen desperately in love with the stranger at first sight.   He seemed to her as an ideal, her affinity, but alas! she remembered her vow! Aurora was in a very disturbed frame of mind when Spencer Hamilton came forward for the encore.

Spencer Hamilton, the violin virtuoso had, in the meantime, another mission to perform in connection with his appearance as a musical artist.   He was no other than Margaret Mac-Donald herself, metamorphosed by Hyder Ben Raaba into the virile, manly fellow who had assumed the name of Spencer Hamilton and, as a violinist, had come to lay siege to the heart of Aurora.

With his furtive glances now and then he was reading the soul of Aurora, now full of perplexing emotions.   He could hardly control his own emotions and began to render as an encore a tune which he expected would create a tumult in the breast of Aurora Cunningham.

Putting forth all his energy so as to make it his best effort in execution, he played to one alone.

At first Aurora thought that the tune had

some vague resemblance to a musical production which she had heard before, but could not tell when and where. As it proceeded it gradually dawned upon her that, somehow there was a connection between the thought of Margaret and the music. She became more and more agitated and was quite certain now that this soul-stirring melody was the creation of her dear, beloved friend and confidant, Margaret MacDonald. Then she realized that the words were her own.

"Oh, the oath!" she gasped, her brain in a delirium of intoxication. Realizing fully that the melody was nothing else than the very composition of Margaret, and that she had written the words at the Diana Seminary on the very eventful night of the moonlight reception, she was unable to conceive how it had become a public property. Was Margaret after all a capricious traitor, a recalcitrant, who had forsaken her solemn vow and desecrated their covenant?

These and other thoughts drove Aurora to the verge of collapse, and as Spencer Hamilton concluded the piece with a finale of deep pathos that reached the pinnacle of tragic intensity, there was commotion around where Aurora was enthroned, for she had lost consciousness.

Thinking that the intense interest and excitement of the occasion had caused her faintness, she was gently removed to her apartment and the program of the evening's festivities was completed with a brilliant reception and dance. Hamilton himself, however, was so affected that he left the reception at once and returned to his hotel and there tried to regain strength for the ordeal that he was planning to carry out next day.

The following morning, at the proper time for calling in India, he left his hostelry and directed his steps toward the Viceregal palace on the pretense of making inquiry concerning the health of Aurora, but ostensibly to reveal the mysterious metempsychosis of himself and to reassert his undying love for her.

Having arrived at the gate he learned that Aurora had been restored to her normal state of health and spirits. He consequently sent in his card and a few minutes later was summoned to the drawing-room of the palace where, after a second's waiting, Aurora Cunningham appeared on the threshold, somewhat flushed and agitated.

Hamilton, on seeing Aurora, came forward and, extending his hand, inquired most anxiously for her health, and intimated that it would give him extreme pleasure to explain certain circumstances which would lead to the gratification of her own unspoken desires.

"I know," he said, "that the encore at last night's musicale affected you very powerfully. I could intuitively read from your perturbed countenance that you had become aware of the authorship of the same.   Aurora, Aurora, I am Margaret MacDonald! I am your confidant at the Diana Seminary, whom you loved, and am now metamorphosed into a man by the miraculous powers of the vivisectionist and reincarnator—Hyder Ben Raaba. I have come to claim you as my own.   Aurora, I love you!"

Aurora, bewildered at this remarkable and dramatic declaration and revelation, too spellbound to speak even a word, uttered a piercing shriek and fell into the open arms of Spencer Hamilton. At the sound of this cry of distress, which echoed throughout the palace, footsteps were heard approaching from every

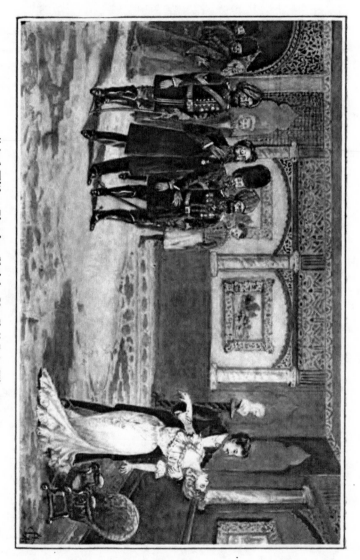

" And With a Piercing Shriek, She Fell Into His Arms "

direction. Soldiers, foot-guards, servants, and the Viceroy Cunningham himself with his guests, rushed into the drawing-room and beheld this highly surprising tableau of romantic love.

Explanations of very delicate and discreet nature were promptly given to the Viceroy by the two lovers, and consent to their union was presently forthcoming.

*　　*　　*　　*

Postscript

After a triumphal bridal tour through England and America, Aurora and Spencer Hamilton settled in the Central African Commonwealth, and by the strenuous qualities inherent in both they had become popular and prominent in civic affairs. Fifteen years later, in 1976, through sheer merit of a public life of usefulness and rectitude, Hamilton was gazetted as Viceroy to the African Commonwealth.

The year 1976 was indeed an epoch-making period. It was the two hundredth anniversary of the Declaration of Independence, and at the same time the semi-centennial of the happy

Anglo-American Alliance. The double jubilee of these two nations, comprising nearly one-half of the world's population, was celebrated wherever the English tongue was spoken, with commensurate grandeur, enthusiasm and eclat, such as absolutely to eclipse all the Durbars, Volkfests and celebrations in the history of the world.

And none the less, the composite but flourishing African Commonwealth, under the wise regime of Spencer Hamilton, was ablaze with prosperous pride in unison with England and America, for this grand and felicitous dual occasion.

[THE END]

LIBRARY
OF THE
UNIVERSITY
OF
CALIFORNIA

CPSIA information can be obtained at www.ICGtesting.com
Printed in the USA
LVOW11*0741240214

374926LV00007B/57/P